"What do you want of me, *monsieur*?"

"Everything," Raoul said promptly. "All that a woman can give to a man."

Halcyon drew back, regretting her question. "That's a tall order!"

"I know it is, but I'm a patient man. I can wait. I usually get what I want."

"Isn't your greatest desire to own the Château des Saules?" she asked deliberately.

A change came over him. The bantering laughter died from his face. He looked around the stone walls of the tower with a brooding gaze. "The price may prove too high," he murmured. "I'm not sure I can pay it."

"Of course you can," Halcyon said, "All that is needed is your signature to a marriage contract."

Crown of Willow

by

ELIZABETH ASHTON

Harlequin Books

TORONTO • LONDON • LOS ANGELES • AMSTERDAM
SYDNEY • HAMBURG • PARIS • STOCKHOLM • ATHENS • TOKYO

Original hardcover edition published in 1975
by Mills & Boon Limited

ISBN 0-373-01946-7

Harlequin edition published February 1976

Second printing November 1977
Third printing September 1980

PRINTED IN U.S.A.

CHAPTER ONE

THE green fronds of the weeping willows drooped towards the water in the stone basin like the long tresses of some nature sprite, the sun shining from a cloudless blue sky spangled the water with shimmering points of light. The basin was in reality an old Roman bath, oblong in shape, surrounded by marble paving and the broken stumps of one-time columns. A screen of cypress trees stood between it and the chateau in the grounds of which it was situated. The chateau had been built on the site of a Roman villa, for France carries many mementoes of her one-time Latin conquerors, and its position was too strategic not to be utilised by subsequent warring factions. It stood upon a little promontory extending into the River Loire, not quite an island, for it was connected with the main land by a narrow isthmus, though sometimes in the flood season it was completely cut off.

But the bath had been of no interest to the chateau's succession of owners, and had become filled with silt and dead leaves, until the present possessor had realised its potential as a swimming pool and had cleaned and repaired it, filling in the cracks in the marble and releasing the clear spring which filled it, the waters of which were drained off by a sluice when they became too high, thus ensuring they were always fresh and cool. But though it had been possible to repair the bath, little remained of its once ornate surroundings.

Only a couple of battered statues, the blind eyes of which sought their reflection in the water. With the drooping willows at one end, it was a peaceful and secluded spot, where on this summer's afternoon past and present met in timeless harmony.

A girl was swimming back and forth in the pool, from which the hot sun had taken the chill. She came there every afternoon after a morning spent helping her father, who was working in the chateau. He was an artist and had been engaged to clean and retouch the pictures in the gallery which ran the length of the first floor of the building. The owners, who had only recently bought the place, were still in Paris, but they would be coming to take up residence later in the summer. Meanwhile Halcyon Grey revelled in the fine old place, and the caretaker, old André, had told her she might make use of the newly renovated pool as often as she chose until the family arrived. Then it would be different, and he proudly showed her the stack of gay umbrellas, canvas chairs and hammocks which would be set up round the pool and under the willows for the comfort of his master and his guests. Then of course Mademoiselle would understand she could not disport herself there without an invitation. Mademoiselle assured him that she understood perfectly, but she expected that by the time Monsieur Dubois and his family arrived, their task in the gallery, if not actually completed, would be nearly so. It was just as well, for the pool was luring her from her own labours, for which she had developed a curious reluctance.

Halcyon Grey had had a modest success with historical romances. Two of her books had been published and she was engaged upon her third. But since she had come to Gracedieu, the village where she and her father were staying, her inspiration had died instead of, as she had hoped, being stimulated. Not that her efforts were profound, her stories were merely the light, bright novels that are favoured by women seeking warmth and colour in their humdrum lives with the main emphasis upon the emotional aspect.

Since coming to France Halcyon had experienced a strange restlessness, an inability to concentrate. Her youth was reaching out for something more tangible than imagined feelings. Though she wrote glibly about love, she had had little in her own life and the heroes she created were unreal beings; the exciting, virile men she sought to portray had no counterpart among the ordinary specimens who had come her way.

As she floated on her back, gazing up into the azure heavens, her mouth twisted wryly. Tall, dark and handsome—the hero's formula, or perhaps not handsome, but arresting, magnetic, certainly different from Louis Perron, the artist who haunted her father's studio in the hope of encountering her, a loose-jointed shambling figure, tall certainly, but with a red wispy beard and untidy hair, neither arresting nor magnetic.

As for her father himself, Felix was a dear, but hopelessly, vague and impracticable. If it had not been for her aunt she would have fared badly, for her mother had died at her birth. Aunt Mildred, a childless widow, had seen to it that her niece was fed, clothed and educated and kept house for her feckless brother who was more often absent than present. Though Halcyon loved her father, he was not the type of man she would ever want to marry. Like many women she secretly yearned to be dominated, to be taken care of instead of having to fend for herself. Now Aunt Mildred was dead and Halcyon and her father were trying to organise their joint lives.

And I'll have to get a move on with that next book, she thought, or the exchequer'll be getting low.

For she was paying the rent of the cottage where they were staying at Gracedieu and it was her energy which had driven her father into accepting the renovation work upon Dubois' pictures. Felix Grey was always on the verge of achieving success, but never quite did so, though several of his pictures had been shown in worthwhile exhibitions, and he occasionally obtained a good price for one. He had lived from hand to mouth while his sister cared for his child, a vague, gentle creature with only two immovable obsessions—he would not give up painting and he could not stay in the same place for long.

Halcyon turned over and swam towards the clump of willow trees at the end of the pool. They overhung the paving to form a natural screen. She hoped the new owners would not cut them down to make room for more sophisticated furnishings and would spare them for their shade. She pulled herself out on to the marble rim of the pool, her eyes still dazzled by the light on the water. The paving stones were warm to her feet as she pattered towards her refuge, dripping as she went. Her regulation-style white swimsuit clung to her limbs so that she looked like one of the statues come to life, for she had only as yet acquired a slight tan. Her wet hair, of a dark auburn tint, hung heavy over her shoulders. She was long-limbed, above average height, with cameo-clear features and delicate wrists and ankles, but she had never been vain and was indifferent to her appearance. Aunt Mildred had instilled into her that blue eyes, fair hair and rosebud mouths were the criterion of beauty, and bemoaned Halcyon's long, greenish-hazel eyes as 'peculiar'.

Halcyon parted the fronds of drooping willow and

her body became rigid with shock. Sprawling beside her discarded slacks and tank top, idly flicking at flies with her towel, was a young man, a man whose description would easily fit the hero of her next romance, for he had all the attributes—bronzed limbs displayed by his short-sleeved open-necked shirt, dark hair curling about a well-shaped head, and eyes tawny as a lion's gazing up at her in insolent appraisal from under dark winged brows that slanted slightly upwards from his straight nose.

But Halcyon was not thinking of romances, she was embarrassed and indignant at this invasion of her privacy and very conscious of her figure defined by the wet bathing dress. That he was conscious of it too and taking stock of it increased her ire.

'Are you aware that you're trespassing, monsieur?' she asked, speaking in English, for her French was not very fluent.

He smiled, a lazy sensuous smile, and his eyelids drooped, veiling the brilliance of his eyes.

'So you are human,' he remarked in the same language, only a slight accent and a more careful enunciation betraying that it was not his native tongue. 'I thought for a moment you were a naiad strayed from the river, or perhaps the ghost of that poor girl for whom the willows are a perpetual memorial.'

Against her will her interest was caught. There must be many legends about such an antique spot, but she had never heard any of them.

'What girl, monsieur? I haven't heard the story.'

'Antoinette de Valprès, the last Comtesse of the Chateau des Saules, who died under the guillotine.'

She had gleaned from her wanderings about the chateau that it had once belonged to a family called de Valprès, who had lost it during the Revolution, and probably Antoinette's portrait was among those she had been renovating, but it was absurd to connect her with the willows.

'I think you're inventing, monsieur; those trees can't be two hundred years old.'

'There have been willows here for a long time, that is why the chateau is named for them, but perhaps the original ones did not weep.'

Halcyon crossed her arms over her bosom and shivered, less with cold than a slight sense of foreboding. This man could only be a stray traveller who had come to view the Roman bath because he knew something of its history, this chance encounter would have no aftermath, but the odd sensation remained, a feeling that something momentous was happening, though how it could be she had no idea.

His next remark was prosaic enough to dispel any fey fancies.

'If you are not a spirit or a water nymph, what are you doing here? This is private property.'

She tossed back her wet hair; preposterous that he, the interloper, should presume to tell her that.

'I've as much right here as you have—more, in fact.'

'I doubt it.'

'I've been given permission to bathe here until the Dubois arrive from Paris.' She paused, eyeing him uncertainly. 'But perhaps you're one of the family?' She had not been present when her father had been interviewed by Pierre Dubois, nor was she sure of how many of them there were. 'In which case...'

He sprang to his feet in a swift, lithe movement which indicated perfect co-ordination of muscles, cutting her short with a vehement ejaculation.

'*Mon Dieu*, never one of those *parvenus*!' Black brows drew together over his haughty nose, while the amber eyes glinted between dark lashes. 'Usurpers,' he muttered angrily. 'Time-servers!' He scowled at the line of cypresses that hid the chateau, all but its tallest towers.

Halcyon stared at him astonished by this outburst, while some inner voice warned her that this would be a dangerous man to cross.

'But this is their land, monsieur,' she said faintly.

'Bought with their ill-gotten wealth.'

'I wouldn't know about that,' she said uneasily, sensing some deep-seated resentment that she did not understand. 'You don't mean they've robbed a bank or something?'

His gaze came back to her and he laughed gaily. 'No, mademoiselle, nothing like that. Perhaps I would think more of Dubois if he had, but he hasn't the guts. Naturally you did not know about it.' He smiled sunnily, shrugging his shoulders. 'It is old history, *ma chère*, a wrong that present circumstances can now correct.'

'Well, I'm glad to hear that,' she said vaguely, wondering what he was talking about.

Standing he had the advantage of her, for he was a head taller than she was. Now she would have to look up to meet his eyes, but she sought to avoid them. There was that in his regard which made her feel acutely self-conscious, though she was not normally bashful. Some physical awareness had sprung up between them, the male in him seeking response from her womanhood. Surreptitiously she observed that his broad shoulders tapered to a slim waist and lean flanks, and his carriage was proud, almost arrogant, due partly to the way his fine head was set on his shoulders and partly to some inborn pride of race. The amber eyes with their fringes of black lashes continued to survey her with a slumbrous sensuality that stirred her femininity. Her brain registered that here was a personality she could identify with a romantic hero ... or a villain, she was not sure which. He was exciting, but a man to be treated with caution.

The willow leaves dappled her with small mauve shadows, stray sunbeams ignited ruddy gleams amid the darkness of her hair, which was nearly dry. She was not aware of the charming picture she made, but her companion was.

'Please may I have my towel?' she asked. He was standing between her and her clothes.

'Your pardon, mademoiselle.' He smiled with a flash of white teeth, a wholly charming smile. Stooping, he picked up the towel, which he held out to her. As she moved to take it, the fingers of his other hand closed over her wrist, and loosening his hold of the towel, he lightly stroked her extended arm with his fingertips. The action was almost a caress, which set her nerves tingling. This man was dynamite.

'How dare you?' she flashed, snatching hand and towel from his clasp.

'I only wish to ascertain that you are really human.'

She wrapped the towel about her. It was a large one and she was thankful for its enveloping folds.

'Of course I'm human,' she returned, hoping he had no idea of how his touch had disturbed her, but not at all sure it had not been calculated. Even so, it was ridiculous to be so susceptible; it must be the result of her continual preoccupation with romance, and she was furious with herself ... and him for allowing herself to be so affected. But never before had she met a man with this one's subtle appeal, nor so good-looking, nor ... he had everything, but she wished he would remove himself so that she could dress.

It seemed he had no intention of doing so. His gaze had dropped to her feet, narrow slender feet, a fitting finish to her long, slender legs. His eyes travelled up them until they reached her face. The fronds of the weeping willow enclosed them in a green mysterious world, enwrapped in the sensuous warmth of a summer's afternoon.

Halcyon met his glance squarely, and saw in the amber depths of his eyes a wondering, almost puzzled expression as he murmured softly:

'A *coup de foudre* ... I would not have believed it were possible.'

'You talk in riddles. There's no thunder about to-day,' she told him a little tremulously, for strange, inexplicable emotions were stirring within her.

'You are wrong, the air is full of electricity. Can't you feel it?'

With an effort she threw off the mesmeric enchantment with which the golden afternoon, their pagan surroundings and her handsome companion were charming her senses and her sanity. He was a complete stranger and she was no impressionable teenager to fall headlong for a personable man upon their first meeting.

'I can't say I do,' she said coldly, 'and I really must be going. If you would be so good as to go away so I can get dressed, I'd be much obliged.'

Her words seemed to recall him to time and place. He glanced down at the garments at his feet and back at her with a mischievous glint in his eyes.

'So my nymph wishes to obscure her beauty in these hideous clothes!' With one toe he touched her slacks. 'I do not know if I can bring myself to allow you to do so.'

'Oh, really, monsieur!' She laughed a little vexedly.

'I can't spend the afternoon in a bath-towel to please your aesthetic taste.'

'Why not? I find your present costume, or rather lack of it, delightful.'

To her annoyance, she felt herself blush. She glanced around, but there was no one in sight. There was unlikely to be at that hour, for old André would be enjoying an afternoon nap, and the Dubois were still in Paris, while her father would have gone back to his studio in the cottage, and would not dream of coming to look for her until it became too dark to paint. What a situation, to be trapped by this tourist, trespasser, tramp ... no, that last he could never be with that face and figure, but that did not make him any less menacing, but rather more dangerous, for her reaction to him was unwillingly responsive.

Drawing herself up with an attempt at dignity, she observed coolly:

'You haven't explained who you are or what you're doing here.'

'Neither have you.'

'I told you I've permission to bathe here while the family are away, and I warn you, old André doesn't care for intruders.'

'Old André is taking a siesta and is dead to the world, as you very well know,' he returned. 'No one is likely to interrupt us, and I am tempted to demand ransom for your clothes.'

Deliberately he moved to stand astride them, while his lips curved mischievously.

'I don't care for cheap gallantry,' she said haughtily, though inwardly she quailed.

Very softly he murmured: 'Perhaps I could make you care.'

A voice low and seductive, the call of a dove to its

14

mate. The narrowed eyes sought her own with an audacious gleam. A man should not be blessed with such gorgeous eyelashes, she thought inconsequently. Her glance dropped to the smooth brown arms, almost she could feel their muscular strength encircling her body. Mentally she shook herself. She must not yield to his sensuous spell. A practised Don Juan, this one, wanting to while away the tedium of a summer's afternoon with a few idle kisses. She stiffened her slight body, drew the towel more securely about her and said coldly:

'Monsieur, you're wasting my time and yours. Will you kindly allow me to retrieve my things?'

His smile was wholly charming.

'Is she really so cold and chaste?' he asked the willow trees. 'Or is she merely seeking to increase my ardour? She does not look frigid.' His eyes dwelt upon her soft mouth with the passionate curve of its lower lip. 'I think you are merely asleep, *chérie*. Let it be my privilege to wake you, *la belle au bois dormant*.'

He took a step towards her, his eyes glowing and Halcyon felt an urge to go to meet him, to let herself drown in his embrace, for that would appear to be his intention, but training and habit re-established themselves. She had never made herself cheap and she was not going to start now, in spite of the overwhelming fascination this man seemed able to exert over her.

She drew back saying sharply:

'No, thank you, I'm fully awake, I assure you, and it isn't a practice of mine to encourage strangers.'

'Am I a stranger to you?' he asked. 'I feel as if I had known you a long time.'

'I've never seen you before in my life!'

'Then perhaps in a former life, we knew each other

15

in the days when this bath was new.'

'A pretty fancy, but I'm afraid I've no recollection of it,' she said cuttingly. She glanced over her shoulder, wondering what André would say if she appeared before him in only a swimsuit and a towel, but she could tell him there was a trespasser by the pool and that he had stolen her clothes.

As if he guessed her thought, the stranger said:

'I could catch you, my nymph, before you gained the chateau.' He smiled mockingly. 'Unless some god turned you into a laurel tree, as Daphne was to escape Apollo and Syrinx turned into a reed to save her from Pan. Perhaps a willow tree would be more appropriate, but you would find that a dull existence. Your face and figure were designed for love, as I would demonstrate if you would permit me to do so. Or is it that some lucky fellow holds your heart and to whom you give the favours you deny to me?'

'You're talking nonsense,' she retorted, 'and I've more important things to do than provide you with an afternoon's diversion. You're right in one thing, another man has a claim upon me, and he'll be wanting his tea!'

He raised one eyebrow in almost comical dismay.

'Tea? *Mon Dieu*, he cannot be a Frenchman!'

'He isn't. He's my father, and if I don't show up soon he'll come to fetch me.'

Which she knew was untrue, but she hoped to intimidate her companion with the threat of a wrathful parent descending upon them.

The stranger shook his black head, while laughter shimmered in his eyes.

'You disappoint me. Tea and fathers and these.' He prodded her slacks with a disdainful toe. 'Desecration upon a day of pagan splendour! *Eh bien*, I suppose I

16

must let you go, but first, may I not have one kiss?'

That was what he had been leading up to, but Halcyon had no intention of submitting, though the thought of his embrace sent a quiver through her body. Pagan was the operative word, he could be Pan or a faun with his laughing eyes and sensual mouth, with the willow tree dappling him with sunbeams and shadow. But he was also a complete stranger and she did not even know his name.

'No,' she said firmly.

'So you will not give, little hard heart? Then I must take.'

He swooped towards her, but as his hand clutched at the towel, she slipped from under it and dived back into the pool.

He would not follow her, she decided, without discarding his elegant pants and shirt, and certainly his shoes, and that would give her time to reach the further side and seek sanctuary in the chateau grounds, where, since she knew the layout and he did not, it should be easy to evade him. But evidently his desire for a kiss was not strong enough to face cold water, for he made no attempt to do so. Probably he had not believed that she meant her denial until she dived into the pool; most good-looking men had a high conceit of themselves and he thought he was irresistible. His voice reached her as she caught at the coping on the further side and turning her head, she saw he was standing on the marble rim and looking very much amused.

'Come back, *chérie*, I swear I will not touch you.'

'I would need to be sure of that,' she returned, hoisting herself on to the edge of the bath. She sat there, dangling her legs over the edge of the rim with the breadth of gleaming water between them.

17

He spread his hands in mock apology.

'I did not intend to drive you back into the pool. I am desolate at your desertion. Come back and tell me your name.'

'You can find that out for yourself, and I prefer to stay where I am until you've gone.'

She did not need to raise her voice, the water carried the sound.

'You do not trust me?'

'Not an inch!'

He laughed gaily. '*Eh bien*, perhaps you are wise. But you have distracted me from the business upon which I came.'

In the bright light she could see the expression on his face, and she saw it change from laughter to sombreness. Suddenly he looked much older and his fine mouth set in lines of determination, as his glance turned from her to the towers of the chateau visible above the screen of cypress trees. Halcyon felt a sudden chill. Was he a thief spying out the land for a planned robbery before the Dubois returned? She must warn André that a suspicious character was lurking in the grounds. Even while the suspicion crossed her mind, he made her a sweeping bow and the shadow was replaced with laughter again.

'*Alors*, I will go now so that you can robe yourself in your ugly *culottes*. Thank you for a charming interlude which would have been entirely delightful if it had ended as it should have done with a kiss. *Eh bien*, it served to take my mind off my troubles. *Adieu*, water nymph.'

He waved his hand and walked away with a swift purposeful stride, and disappeared between the cypress trees without a backward glance.

Halcyon waited, wondering if he had really gone,

18

but nothing stirred in the drowsy afternoon heat. She rubbed her eyes, wondering if she had fallen asleep and the whole episode had been a dream, but in that case what was she doing on the wrong side of the pool? She dropped back into the water, swam across, climbed the opposite edge, and picked up her towel, ears and eyes alert for a tall graceful figure lounging towards her and footsteps on the marble brink. Cautiously she parted the willow fronds, half expecting to find him there, but only emptiness met her gaze and the buzzing of a vagrant bee. Hastily she dried herself and put on her clothes. Then she paused, irresolute. Should she go and warn André that there was a prowler in the grounds? She found she was reluctant to do so. She might be only alarming the old man unnecessarily if the stranger had no sinister intentions. Yet he had indicated that he had come with some purpose, which might or might not be innocent.

By the slant of the sun she knew the afternoon must be well advanced and her father would be expecting the welcome break of a cup of tea, for they lunched early after their return from their morning's work at the chateau. She looked round her green refuge with a curious sense of deprivation. Naturally she was relieved that the stranger had gone without forcing upon her his unwelcome demonstrations, but the place seemed empty without his vibrant presence. He had said he had felt he had known her always and she had taken his words to be an opening gambit towards intimacy only a little less corny than the usual, 'Haven't we met before?' But he had also spoken of a *coup de foudre*, a clap of thunder, a French equivalent, she remembered now, for love at first sight. A still more subtle approach?

Impatiently she parted the willow fronds and moved

away from the pool. Her imagination was working overtime, stimulated by this unexpected encounter with a man who could so easily have impersonated one of her romantic heroes. In reality he was nothing of the sort. A hero, however strangely he behaves, must have a fundamental integrity, and not only had he taken advantage of her predicament to while away a tedious hour of waiting, but he might be no better than a common thief. She was foolish to feel sentimental about him and she must put André upon his guard before she went home.

Passing through the cypresses, she came upon a stretch of formal garden that had been laid out around the chateau, parterres of well-disciplined blooms intersected by narrow gravel paths and tiny box hedges. The gardeners had been hard at work planting out ready for the owners' coming. The chateau stood to her left, raised on a rocky eminence, the gravelled road which crossed the garden, ending in a broad flight of steps that led on to a wide terrace, laid out before the imposing entrance doorway. Her way was on the right, where the drive crossed the narrow neck of land that connected the chateau with the mainland.

She started towards the chateau, looking small and a little lost among so much grandeur, swinging her towel and swimsuit from one hand. She was good friends with André who, normally a little gruff and grim, had taken a fancy to the English girl, who was so interested in the Chateau des Saules, which comprised his world. She had only taken a few steps when she stopped abruptly. She had caught sight of two figures upon the terrace, one of which she recognised as André by his white beard and old-fashioned panama hat; the other was the stranger. They were talking animatedly and she thought she could distinguish the stranger's laugh.

Halcyon turned quickly away and hurried homeward, hoping she had not been perceived. She had gained the impression that the intruder, whoever he was, was no stranger to André.

CHAPTER TWO

The village of Gracedieu where the Greys were spending the summer stood a little higher than the chateau and behind it were rolling hills that grew gradually higher towards the Massif Central from whence the Loire descended through gorges that bore little resemblance to its languid progress through level lands when its course turned westward. Nevers was a smudge on the horizon, a manufacturing town, where among more utilitarian products a porcelain faience industry still flourished. It was vineyard country, and vines were cultivated amid forest and pasture lands. Halcyon had hoped to collect copy for her next book, which dealt with the great days of the First Empire. She had collected data in Paris, and this part of France, where the departments of Berry, Champagne and Burgundy were adjacent should be rich in atmosphere for her country scenes. Today she had met with more than scenery, an individual who had stimulated her imagination, though it would tax her pen to describe the virile essence of the man by the pool that was both provocative and seductive. Naturally her creations were not portraits of living people, in any case that was not permissible, but a voice or a face glimpsed in a crowd often fired her invention, and she built her characters accordingly. The brave and honourable Capitaine Jacques of her book could have little in common with the slick opportunist she had met that afternoon, and she wondered what tale he had spun to André and whether she should have gone to the old man's support.

Tall, rather dingy houses lined the cobbled main street of the village, with the inevitable washing strung from window to window. In the centre of the village was a dusty square, where a market was held once a week. The over-large church was to one side, administrative offices on the other. In the centre was an ancient well with plane trees planted round it from which the villagers still drew water with a bucket on a windlass though most of the houses now had stand pipes.

Halcyon crossed the *place* and wended her way along the main road which continued beyond it. The last house at its furthest point was where she was staying, and was coyly called 'Le Nid'. It was actually a one-storeyed bungalow of later date than most of the village houses though no richer in amenities. It was surrounded by a rail fence. The front door opened into a narrow passage which bisected the house. The larger of the two front rooms was her father's studio, with a north light skylight installed by a former artist tenant. He kept the window shuttered to exclude the sunlight when he was working. The room opposite to it was his bedroom and behind it was hers. The other room at the back was the kitchen, where they took their meals. It had a red-tiled floor, a dutch dresser which held the crockery, an oil cooker and a charcoal brazier for warmth. This last was set in an old-fashioned fireplace with an iron pot suspended above it on a hook. This was their only means of heating washing water. In the middle of the room was a wooden table, its top scoured white with many scrubbings.

Altogether it was a primitive little place, but Halcyon liked it. They had rented it for the summer from a Monsieur Blum, who told them it was much in demand by visitors seeking a quiet retreat, but he had a liking for artists, and the bungalow had been designed for the needs of such. The rent being moderate, they had taken it with relief. It was the first real home Halcyon had ever had. Her aunt's house had always seemed alien.

The baker had left a long loaf on the front doorstep, and collecting it, she went round to the back—they rarely used the front entrance—and found the door ajar with a familiar figure in shabby jeans and shirt making himself very much at home. She sighed, for she was in no mood for company, and least of all Louis Perron's, for though ostensibly a friend and colleague of her father's he was beginning to present a personal problem.

He was of mixed parentage, his mother being English, and had given up his prospects in his father's firm to pursue his art. He lived in a tent and painted small pictures of the chateaux in the vicinity which he sold to the souvenir shops in the towns along the Loire. He did not usually stay long in one place, but had lingered in Gracedieu, saying it was so pleasant to meet a fellow artist, but Halcyon more than suspected that she was the attraction. Since it was by no means reciprocated, she found him something of a bore. In appearance he was the typical drop-out with long reddish hair and a wispy beard, and when she had first met him, not over-clean. He had become more particular since knowing her and not only washed but occasionally trimmed his hair and beard.

Since Felix was at home he had found the back door unlocked, but he knew better than to disturb his friend when at work. Halcyon saw he had lit the

Primus and the kettle was nearly boiling.

'I thought you would be ready for a cup of tea when you came in,' he told her, while his pale blue eyes lit up at the sight of her. He spoke English, thanks to his mother, like a native.

'Thank you, but please let me make it,' Halcyon requested, for Louis, like many of the French, was never very successful with tea-making.

She reached for the brown earthenware teapot reposing on a shelf, while he clumsily tried to forestall her. They collided and she hastily drew away from him. A hurt look came into the pale eyes.

'You don't like me much, do you, Hal?'

'Of course I like you,' she said a little testily, for she had had enough of amorous males for one afternoon, and this one was not prepossessing. 'But I'm not sentimental. Look, the kettle is boiling.' She hurriedly made the tea.

'But you're often cruel to me,' he complained.

'Not intentionally, you're too sensitive. Will you call Daddy or shall I?'

'There, you see, you can't bear to be alone with me.'

'But it's late and Daddy will want his tea,' she told him patiently, throwing a red and white check tablecloth over the table. 'It would help if you got down the cups and saucers.' She indicated the dresser and went into the tiny annexe behind the kitchen which contained the sink and a stone slab, on which she kept the milk and butter. In the absence of a fridge it was the coolest place for them.

When she returned she found Felix had not waited to be called. Louis was obediently laying the table, but her father had cut the end off the long loaf and was devouring it hungrily.

'Really, Daddy, are you so starved you couldn't

wait?' she remonstrated.

He grinned at her, and reaching for the butter, liberally plastered his hunk of bread with it.

'I've been struggling with that darned picture of the chateau Dubois commissioned,' he explained, 'and that made me feel famished. The beastly thing is coming along at last and I hope Monsieur is pleased with it.'

'Which you're not?' Louis queried, sitting down to the table, while Halcyon proceeded to pour out. The meal was simple—bread, butter, jam and a cake of her own making.

'I hate that kind of picture, mere photography,' Felix went on. 'He'll expect every detail depicted, even the dog kennel, if there were a dog kennel, but my daughter insisted that I did it. She's a slave-driver, Louis.'

'He offered you a very good price for it,' Halcyon pointed out. 'Much more than you get for one of your abstracts. We could do with the money.'

'Hal, you've no soul!'

'Someone has to be practical. I don't believe in starving in the gutter for the sake of an idea.'

'It's the same with me,' Louis said wistfully. 'To eat, I have to paint what the tourists will buy.'

Felix gave him a derisive look but said nothing. Being an infinitely superior artist to the younger man, he thought Louis was lucky to be able to sell anything.

'André tells me the Dubois family are due to arrive this evening,' he announced, and catching Halcyon's surprised look, added, 'They phoned after you'd gone for your swim.'

'That's very sudden,' she exclaimed, 'and we haven't finished the pictures.'

'Apparently that spoilt puss, his daughter, had a

sudden longing for the country, which being translated means that her favourite beau has escaped down here, or she has exhausted her preserves and is seeking pastures new.'

'And they say women are catty,' Halcyon murmured. 'What has she ever done to you?'

'You haven't met her yet.' Felix had been interviewed by the Dubois family before he had been engaged to renovate the picture gallery, but Halcyon had not been with him. 'But their coming won't disturb us, though I'm afraid you'll have to keep within bounds.'

Halcyon sighed. That meant no more bathing in the Roman bath, nor could she roam over the chateau at will as André had allowed her to do. She had gazed in wonder at the huge salon with its swathed furniture and glass chandeliers and climbed the narrow crooked stairs to the top of each of the twin towers to admire the fine view from their summit. She remarked as she poured her father a second cup of tea:

'It's a big place for only three of them.'

'Oh, they'll be entertaining, and the daughter, Mariette, is to have a ball to celebrate her birthday, which I gather is to be a great event, in fancy dress too. You could help them with that, you know something about period costume.'

'I don't suppose they'd need to consult me, and I don't know a lot.' Her historical researches had taught her what clothes her characters would wear.

'You'll know a darned sight more than they will.' He gulped his tea. Setting down the cup, he remarked: 'Incidentally, when I undertook to paint the chateau, Dubois did hint that he would like me to do a portrait of his precious Mariette.'

'Really? Then if he mentions it again, mind you jump at it.'

Felix spread his hands despairingly.

'Hal, what have I done to deserve such a punishment? You know he'll expect a conventional likeness.'

'Which you can do to perfection if you set your mind to it. You know we can't afford to be choosy.'

'I told you she was a slave-driver,' Felix said to Louis.

'Why do you submit?' the younger man asked reproachfully. 'I wouldn't sell my independence to an ignorant plutocrat!'

Father and daughter exchanged glances; both knew poor Louis would be only too glad to accept such a commission if it were offered to him. There was a strong family likeness between the two of them. They had the same large, intelligent eyes, more green than hazel, but whereas Halcyon's hair was dark auburn, Felix's beard and thinning locks were light brown.

'You haven't got a daughter to support,' Felix pointed out, though this was hardly correct. He never had wholly supported Halcyon and she paid her share of their present household expenses.

'The bondage of family ties,' Louis exclaimed a little wildly. 'I've repudiated them.' He got to his feet. 'Thank you for the tea, Hal, but I'll be getting on my way while you gloat over the fortune you'll make out of Dubois.'

'Hardly that,' Felix was beginning, when the young man stumped out of the door. 'What's bitten him?' he asked, bewildered.

'Jealousy,' Halcyon returned, 'and the fact that he can't afford to keep a wife.'

Felix whistled. 'So that's the way the land lies. I rather thought it did. Do I congratulate you upon a conquest?'

'You do not. It's a complication I don't want.'

'If he's smiiten hard enough, he might make it up with his father,' Felix said thoughtfully. 'Perron would take him back if he'd promise to conform, and as it is, I believe his mother subsidises him on the Q.T. You might find life with him more rewarding than burdening yourself with an ageing parent.'

She laid her hand over his on the table. 'Never a burden, Daddy. I'm much happier with you than ever I'd be with Louis, however affluent he became.'

'I've been a poor father to you, Hal.'

'You've done what you could,' she squeezed his fingers affectionately.

'But some day I'll make it all up to you. Eventually I'll be recognised. I must be.'

Halcyon smiled indulgently. He dreamed of future fame, and it was his justification for living for his art and leaving her to be brought up by her aunt, but she was doubtful if he would ever attain it. Meanwhile he made a bare living and she was happy to be with him, while her own earnings promised to increase, in which case she could supply the jam to sweeten their daily bread.

The mention of the Dubois' arrival took her mind back to her meeting with the young man by the pool. Could he have been a guest arriving in advance of his host? In that case she might meet him again when she went to the chateau. Briefly she gave her father an expurgated account of that encounter, but all he said was:

'I'm afraid you won't be able to bathe there any more now the family is back.'

'I know that.'

'Not that they really appreciate the place, they'd be much happier at Le Touquet. Dubois only bought it because he imagines its possession gives him prestige.

The portraits we're so assiduously cleaning aren't his ancestors.'

During the ravages of the last war, the pictures had been stowed away, possibly in the old dungeons, for some of them were mildewed. The chateau had been used as a hospital, and had only comparatively recently come on the market. Dubois had spent a lot of money upon its renovation.

'Has he no connection with the original family?'

'None whatever, he's a thorough *parvenu*, though he tries to pretend there is. Before the Revolution the Chateau des Saules belonged to the Comte de Valprès, but I don't know if he left any descendants.'

'I don't think he did.' She was remembering what her acquaintance by the Roman bath had said, 'I ... someone told me ... the last de Valprès perished on the guillotine.'

'Bad luck, but their ghosts must be riled to see Dubois in possession.'

'If there are any.' But had not the stranger told her she might be the wraith of the unfortunate Antoinette? Antoinette for whom the green willow was a lasting memorial. But who had planted them, and who had mourned her? That she would never know, though if she did meet the man of the bathing episode again, he might be able to enlighten her.

Felix went back to his painting and after she had cleared the meal, Halcyon wandered out into the small square of garden behind the house. She could see the tops of the towers belonging to the chateau beyond the village, towers that had seen so many years of history, and had now become a rich man's plaything. As well the de Valprès had died out and there was no one left to be galled by its passing from their proud ownership.

Halcyon went with her father next morning to the chateau filled with curiosity to meet its owners. Pierre Dubois came to them when they had been working for a little while. The renovated portraits, cleaned and revarnished, were back on the walls, their heavy frames re-gilded and repaired. Those still to be done stood on the floor, their faces towards the wainscoting. Halcyon was varnishing one of a gentleman in brocaded coat and powdered wig. He had, she noticed, a thin aquiline face and almost yellow eyes. As she stared at it, it seemed to her the features were vaguely familiar, then recognising her fancy, she almost laughed. She must be quite obsessed with the man she had met yesterday if she imagined she was seeing him again in the portrait of this long-dead de Valprès.

Pierre Dubois was short, fat and round-faced, and tried to make himself appear more distinguished by wearing an imperial. He had black beady eyes, but they were shrewd. He looked with approval at their work, rubbing his pudgy hands together.

'Excellent, *mon ami*. Now we can see what those ancestors of mine really looked like!'

Felix said nothing, and surprising a quizzical gleam in his eyes, Dubois went on hurriedly:

'I am distantly connected with the de Valprès, you know, so I have every right to claim them as ancestors.'

'Of course, Monsieur Dubois,' Felix agreed, thinking that if there really was a connection it would have been on the wrong side of the blanket.

Dubois turned his eyes towards Halcyon. 'Your daughter?'

'Yes, monsieur. She is assisting me.'

'She also paints?'

'No, monsieur, her talents lie in other directions. She is a historical scholar and knows a lot about period costume.'

'Ah, splendid!' The little man beamed at Halcyon. 'Mademoiselle, you will be able to assist with our *bal masqué*, which is to be an *affaire magnifique*.' He proceeded to enlarge upon the splendours he envisaged, while Halcyon wished her father had held his tongue. She had no desire to help with this ball, and she suspecting he was paying her back for her insistence that he must paint Mariette's picture.

Pointing to the portrait Halcyon was working upon, Dubois said he had thought of copying it for his own costume, and she nearly cried out, 'Sacrilege', but they had almost decided to confine their efforts to the First Empire, when dresses were a little different, were they not?

Halcyon agreed they were, and her father chuckling said:

'Hal has made a special study of that era, and you would make an excellent Napoleon, monsieur.'

Dubois looked gratified, and then passed on to the subject of his daughter's portrait, which he hoped Felix would undertake. It would look well at the end of the long line of de Valprès—a revealing remark, which struck Halcyon as a little pathetic. Knowing his family to be inferior, he hoped by dressing it up to gain equality with the chateau's original owners.

With a grimace that only Halcyon saw, Felix said he would be delighted to paint Mademoiselle Dubois' portrait and stated an exorbitant sum, evidently hoping the proud father would demur, but Dubois accepted it without a quibble.

'I will fetch her, and we can arrange about sittings,' he announced, and hurried away down the long gallery calling, 'Mariette!'

'You're committed now, Daddy,' Halcyon said, 'and

I never thought he'd accept your price.'

Felix grinned. 'Neither did I, but if I've got to endure this penance, at least I'll be well recompensed!'

Mariette was better looking than her father's appearance had led Halcyon to suppose. Though like him she was small, plump, black-haired and black-eyed, her features were regular, and her skin a matt white that looked like satin, though the colour on lips and cheeks was obviously artificial. She had a compact comeliness, her short limbs ending in tiny hands and feet, which made Halcyon feel her own long slender limbs were coltish. Mariette Dubois suggested a Dresden doll.

'So you paint my picture, monsieur?' she said, smiling coquettishly up at the tall artist. 'You will make me look beautiful, *n'est-ce pas?*'

'I can't improve upon nature,' Felix returned guardedly.

She took it as a compliment. When she smiled she dimpled charmingly. Felix could have had a much worse model, Halcyon decided.

This smile vanished as Mariette glanced towards the other girl, and took in her slim grace, the sunlight finding ruddy lights in her dark hair.

'*Votre fille*, monsieur?'

'Yes, my daughter, Halcyon.'

'Halcyon? What a strange name.'

'It was her mother's fancy.'

'There is a story perhaps, monsieur?' Mariette had a child's love of fairy tales.

'It's classical. Halcyon's husband was drowned, and in her grief she threw herself into the sea, and the gods turned her into a bird.'

'Me, I would not like to be called after anything so sad.'

Halcyon wondered, not for the first time, if her mother's choice of name had been a premonition in reverse. Felix had been left a grieving widower.

'And pagan too,' Mariette went on. 'A Saint's name would have been more suitable.'

'Unfortunately you were not there to advise us,' Felix told her a little drily, resenting the criticism.

'You jest, monsieur, naturally I was not there. I am, I should say, much younger than Mademoiselle.' She said it as though Halcyon were at least thirty.

'Possibly,' Felix agreed, and turned to her father.

Mariette continued to stare at Halcyon through half-closed eyes. For some reason she seemed to be resenting her.

'You are staying at Gracedieu, mademoiselle?'

'Yes, looking after my father.'

'It might be better while he is painting me if he stayed at the chateau.'

'I don't think he would like that.'

'Why not? It is an honour to be a guest at the Chateau des Saules.'

'I'm sure it is, but he wouldn't be a guest exactly.'

'He would be if I ask him and he would have no distractions while he worked.'

'You had better put it to him,' Halcyon suggested, confident of her father's refusal. Inexplicably Mariette wanted to separate them, probably in the hope that Halcyon would leave the village, but she could not see how her presence there could affect the spoilt daughter of the chateau. She did not know that short Mariette longed to be tall and lissom and Halcyon's appearance was therefore an affront to her. Moreover, she had an intuition that she had met a rival in some future situation. Halcyon, oddly enough, had a similar feeling, though how could she ever come in conflict with a girl who moved in a totally different sphere?

She thought in romantic jargon, this would be the other woman, but to be the other woman there must be a man, and the only bone of contention between them was her poor father, who was hardly a romantic figure. Involuntarily her mind went to the man she had met by the pool, who had been a romantic figure. Him she was unlikely to meet again and he was unknown to Marietta—or was he? Was he staying at the chateau and had he mentioned her to the other girl? Both speculations were improbable but neither were impossible. They would account for Mariette's obvious antagonism.

The idea that her acquaintance of the pool might be under the same roof with her and she might run into him at any moment caused her pulses to quicken in a quite ridiculous manner. She found herself glancing down the vista of the gallery as if she expected him to materialise at any moment. Then chiding herself for her foolishness, for if he did come it would be Mariette he would be seeking, she set to work upon the picture she was holding, only to be confronted by mocking golden eyes under black brows with an upward tilt at the outer corners.

I must have got a touch of the sun, she mused, as Mariette turned away to chatter to Felix. My imagination is running away with me as usual. Next I'll be supposing that vagabond was a scion of the de Valprès!

But the idea once conceived was not easily dismissed. He could have been a member of that dispossessed family come to view his old home, a descendant of a distant branch that had survived. She remembered how he had called the Dubois usurpers and the bitter expression upon his face, and felt the triumph of a detective who has unearthed a promising clue.

Beyond Louis Perron, whom her father had known before they came to Gracedieu, the Greys had few acquaintances in the neighbourhood, and Halcyon's French was too limited to permit of easy gossip with the shopkeepers, most of whom spoke a sort of patois that was baffling. So they had only scant knowledge of the people living near them. There were vintners and farmers, some of them prosperous, but the Greys had not met them. Perhaps the remnants of the de Valprès family were actually located in the vicinity.

But where does that get me? she considered. Nowhere at all. If he is a de Valprès he wouldn't be invited here, and now the family are back he won't come near the place since he obviously resented them so much. So it's no good hoping to run into him again. Hoping indeed! After his behaviour by the pool that was the last thing that she wanted to do, though an unruly corner of her mind suggested he had been exciting. She varnished the insolent face in the picture with vindictive energy. That to you, Monsieur de Valprès! she thought.

'Hal, have you gone to sleep? I've spoken to you three times and you didn't hear me.'

Halcyon recollected herself with a start. The Dubois had gone. Vaguely she recalled seeing them go. Her father was eyeing her with amusement.

'If I hadn't your assurance to the contrary, I should say you were in love with poor old Louis.'

Halcyon flushed vividly.

'I'd merely lost myself in a new plot for a story,' she explained.

'And like all good romantic novelists, you've fallen for your hero even though he is your own creation?'

Halcyon laughed. 'Well, of course.'

36

Felix sighed.

'Lucky you. I find it impossible to feel sentimental about my new model.'

'Why not? She's a pretty little thing, and from what I saw, quite ready to be flirtatious.'

'My God, Hal, she had a completely empty face!'

Halcyon laughed again at his pained expression.

'Perhaps it's as well you don't find her attractive. It might end disastrously since she's flesh and blood, unlike my hero, who is nebulous.'

Or was he?

CHAPTER THREE

AFTER lunch Felix went somewhat unwillingly back to the Chateau des Saules to keep his first assignment with his model. Dubois had insisted that there was no time like the present and later on Mariette would be busy with the preparations for her birthday ball and would be unable to spare much time to sit for him.

Debarred from the swimming pool, Halcyon felt at a loose end, and it was too nice a day to stay indoors. She decided to go for an exploratory walk, for so far she had seen little of the countryside, spending all her leisure in the chateau grounds.

She started along the road leading out of the village, it edged the river and was lined with the inevitable poplars. It was dusty and hot, with frequent speeding cars, but after covering about half a mile she came to a spot where a tributary of the Loire came down through a steepish gorge with a narrow track beside it. She turned thankfully off the highway to pursue this path. Far in the distance she could see the fretted peaks of the outriding hills of the Massif Central. The air was sharper and clearer as she climbed out of the valley and the rushing water beside her was purer than the river it was hurrying to join. She wished she had brought her bathing suit, for its coolness was tantalising and there were places where it formed deep pools where she could have submerged herself.

However, there was no reason why she should not

soak her tired feet in its limpid depths. Coming to a promontory of rock that overhung one of these pools, she walked to the edge of it, noticing with disgust that even in this remote spot there were signs of human passage. A few rusting tins and a broken bottle had been discarded by Philistines who had picnicked at some time in the area, and she had to keep a sharp look out for broken glass.

Reaching the edge of the rock, she discarded her sandals—she wore neither tights nor stockings—and sat down with her bare legs dangling over it and her feet in the water. It was deliciously refreshing, and since there were no signs of any other visitors—it was too early in the year for them—she could give herself up to enjoyment of her solitude.

A butterfly skimmed past, a kingfisher darted across the water, a streak of vivid blue. Far overhead a lark was singing as it soared into the air. It was a scene of sylvan peace without a discordant note. Leaning forward from her rock, Halcyon stared into the clear stream beneath her, wondering if there were trout in the river.

The sound of hooves and the metallic jingle of a bit caused her to turn her head to look behind her, and she saw a rider on a big black horse coming down the path. Since she was seated at a little distance from it and could present no sort of obstruction, she did not move, but the animal chose to take exception to her presence. It shied violently, nearly unseating its rider, who muttered imprecations beneath his breath, but instead of going on when he had calmed it, he slid from its back, holding it by the reins, which he threw over its head, and regarded the interloper sternly. Halcyon rose to her feet and found herself face to face with the vagrant of the Roman bath. Yellow shirt, beautifully tailored breeches ending in highly polished boots set off his slim athletic figure, a black Spanish hat protected his eyes and neck from the bright sun, in the shadow of which he appeared to be frowning.

Halcyon felt she was hardly to blame if his horse was too frisky, and she was glad that she was not wearing the trousers to which he had objected so strongly. But her green shift-style dress was skimpy and her hair was hanging over her shoulders, which together with her bare legs and feet presented a somewhat undress appearance.

The man's face cleared, and he swept off his hat. '*Alors*, the water nymph again!' he exclaimed. 'No wonder Saracen shied. You vary your habitat, mademoiselle.'

'I'm banished from the willow tree and the Roman bath now the owners have returned,' she told him. 'But this time you can't accuse me of trespassing.'

His lips parted in a flashing smile, she had forgotten how charming it was, and he said teasingly:

'Only if you keep to the path. The fishing in the stream is private.'

'But I wasn't fishing, monsieur. You can see I have no rod.'

'Sure you were not trying to tickle the trout with your toes?'

'Are there trout? I couldn't see any.'

'There are, also snakes.' She flinched and he laughed. 'But maybe they are only eels.'

Light bantering words, but beneath them something much more profound. Halcyon was again almost painfully aware of this man's intense vitality, which made him so attractive. She had not met many men, and never one like this one. He possessed grace and dignity in every line of his supple body, but his appraising

40

gaze under the uptilted brows was as disconcerting as she had found it by the pool. She must be looking a sketch and she was very conscious of her bare legs.

'Perhaps you were, as your English poet says, in maiden meditation, fancy free,' he suggested.

'I was certainly meditating.'

'But are you fancy free?'

She smiled provocatively; her fancy was very much involved with the man before her, but that naturally she would not confess.

'That's telling,' she said archly.

She was rapidly reassessing her first impression of him. He appeared to be a native of the place and a man of means, judging by his clothes and his mount. Yet she had never heard him mentioned during her stay at Gracedieu, but then the villagers were a close-mouthed lot where foreigners were concerned. He was still studying her, taking in her delicate complexion, lightly tanned as yet, her long graceful limbs, and again his regard became fixed upon the promise of her mouth. He stood between her and the path, and she moved restlessly under his assessment, feeling her colour rise.

'Such a charming *jeune fille* is unlikely to be unattached,' he said discontentedly. 'You have left some lovesick swain behind in England?'

'Perhaps.'

'*Eh bien*, perhaps you could be made to forget him. Meanwhile, you too have been dispossessed.'

'Hardly that, I hadn't really any right there.'

'Except that the trailing willow provided an ideal setting for you.'

She hardly heard him, for she was mulling over the significance of that 'too'. Did he also consider himself dispossessed? Recalling her musings of the morning,

41

she asked him greatly daring:

'Are you by any chance a de Valprès?'

A shadow crossed his face. 'Now why should you think that?'

'Because I spent this morning renovating a portrait that was something like you, monsieur.'

'So that is who you are, the painter's daughter. I might have guessed.'

'You've heard of us?'

'*Naturellement*,' he drawled. 'We know all that goes on at Gracedieu. In fact you rented your cottage from my agent.'

He was a man of property even if he did not own the Chateau des Saules.

'I didn't know that,' she told him. 'I thought it belonged to Monsieur Blum. Is he your agent?'

'*Mais oui*, so you know now I am your landlord.' He did not look very pleased about it, and she wondered if he did not approve of his agent's action in letting the cottage to foreigners. Housing was short in France, like everywhere else, and perhaps he thought it should have gone to some local family. She said defensively:

'We're only there for the summer.'

'But what will you do when you have finished the gallery?'

'My father has just been commissioned to paint a portrait of Mademoiselle Dubois.'

'Ah, the so well-endowed Mariette.' He smiled, but this time it was not a charming smile, there was something wolfish about it. 'And have you met her yet?'

'Yes, this morning.'

'A plump *petit pigeon, n'est-ce pas?*'

She smiled at the description. 'She could be called that.'

He looked away towards the distant mountains.

'And pigeons are made to be plucked.'

The words and his expression brought a sudden chill to Halcyon's heart. Mariette was an only child, so that if this man wanted to reinstate himself, the way was easy. Dubois would probably consider it a suitable match, for de Valprès, if he were de Valprès, could give to Mariette the lineage that she lacked in return for her heritage. The thought of them together was oddly distasteful to her, though there was no reason why she should mind. Both were strangers to her and their matrimonial arrangements nothing to do with her.

She shifted from one bare foot to the other, disturbed by her thoughts and anxious to bring this meeting to an end.

'Monsieur, I should be returning and I'm sure your horse is growing impatient.'

For Saracen was tossing his head and pulling at the reins.

'Always you wish to flee from me,' her companion complained.

'I can't stand here much longer, the rock is hard on my feet.'

'Then why do you not put on your sandals?'

She was holding them by their straps in one hand, but that obvious and homely action seemed impossible under his close scrutiny. Instinctively she was on the defensive.

'If I did not have to hold this brute, I would do it for you,' he announced.

Scorning herself for her foolishness, she said hastily:

'Oh, that's not necessary,' and bent down to put on her footgear. Something moved on the rock beside her, it was only a venturesome lizard, but he had mentioned snakes, and she started back, unwary of her going. She gave a cry as a piece of broken glass penetrated her foot.

'It's nothing,' she declared, as he started towards her, dragging the horse after him. She thrust her foot into her sandal, wincing with pain.

'Don't be a fool,' he said tersely. 'It is bleeding badly.'

He turned away and began to lead the horse down the path, so that for a moment she thought he meant to desert her, and felt a flash of resentment. It amused him to tease her, but when he saw she was in real trouble he hastened to make himself scarce. But she had wronged him, for he stopped at the nearest tree and secured Saracen to it.

Halcyon sat down upon a nearby boulder and stared in dismay at the blood oozing between her foot and the sole of her sandal. It must be quite a deep cut. Taking out her handkerchief with some idea of staunching its flow, she hesitated; perhaps it would be better to leave the sandal on and hope its pressure would act as a pad to stop it. She became aware of hurrying footsteps, and realised she had not been deserted. He slipped on his knees beside her, and seized her ankle without ceremony, stripping off her sandal. He held her foot up to examine the wound, and with an instinct of modesty, she clutched at her scanty skirt to prevent it riding up her thighs. The glass had made a ragged incision in the sole of her foot and it was still bleeding profusely. Halcyon felt a tremor run through her body at the touch of those lean brown fingers, which to her horror were soon smeared with red.

'A nasty cut,' he observed. 'It should be bathed.'

Releasing his hold, he stood up and looked about him, and pounced upon his hat which he had dropped carelessly upon the rock. Picking it up, he said to her:

'*Maintenant*, mademoiselle, please not to move from that stone, while I procure some water.'

'I'm in your hands,' she told him faintly, for she was feeling a little sick.

'*Bon*.' He swung himself over the edge of the little promontory with agile ease, while Halcyon watched him stupidly fighting with her nausea. His return was a little more difficult, for he had only one hand for the climb, as he held the hat by its joined brim in the other. As it was, he caught his hand on a jut of rock and spilled a few drops of the precious fluid, inflicting a scratch across below his knuckles. Reaching her, he again knelt and taking her handkerchief from her nerveless grasp, dabbed the wound with the cold water. A few drops of blood from his own scratch mingled with hers.

The scene wavered before Halcyon's eyes; it seemed utterly unreal, the man kneeling at her feet, his black head bent, intent upon his task, the skin of her foot looking fragile and pale against the deep tan of his hands and wrists from which he had rolled back the sleeves, the discoloured water dripping on to the ground, almost as if they were taking part in some mystic rite to which the impatient stamping of the big black horse was an ominous accompaniment. She laughed nervously and said:

'That hat should be a witch's cauldron and its contents a magic potion.'

Thinking she was a little lightheaded, and dubious about his makeshift for a bowl, he told her:

'That hat is perfectly clean, it is new, I wore it for the first time this morning.' He dabbed the scratch on his hand.

Fantasy vanished as Halcyon exclaimed in consternation:

45

'You've ruined a new hat and hurt yourself just to help me?'

'*N'importe*,' he said carelessly. He looked up at her from his ministration with a mischievous gleam in his amber eyes. 'We have mingled blood, which is the most important part of the gipsy rite of marriage.'

'Oh.' She was disconcerted, but she had been correct when she had sensed there was something pagan about their situation. 'I . . . I don't know much about gipsies,' she faltered.

'Neither do I, but I gleaned that information some-where and it just recurred to me.'

He rinsed his hands in the remains of the water and produced a clean handkerchief from his pocket which he bound about her foot.

'To come down to practical matters, that will have to do for now. When you reach home you must wash it thoroughly in disinfectant, since I am afraid the stream possesses no magical properties.'

'You must think I'm a little mad,' she said ruefully, 'it was just . . .' She broke off, unable to explain herself.

'Only a little fey, which is suitable to a water nymph.'

'Pity I'm not one, then I wouldn't bleed,' she ob-served, gazing woefully at the sodden ruin of his hat. 'I . . . I don't know how to thank you.'

He sat back on his heels with a sensuous glint in his eyes, but Halcyon was looking anywhere but at him. She was not normally shy, but something about this man filled her with confusion. She wished it had been anybody else who had succoured her, for she did not wish to be indebted to him, vaguely aware that there might be repercussions with which she could not cope, and his next words were not reassuring.

'I could suggest an easy way to do that. Tell me, are

you one of the permissive girls we hear to much about who have revolutionised British juvenile society?'

The words and their implication gave her an unpleasant jolt.

'Certainly not!' she exclaimed hastily.

'Forgive me,' he said with mock humility, 'I did not mean to insult you, but since you move in artistic circles...' He shrugged his shoulders expressively. *Mais malheureusement,* it is as I feared.'

'Feared?' she asked indignantly.

He spread his hands in a French gesture.

'If you are a *jeune fille très gentille* it makes it much more difficult.'

'I don't understand.' But she did. He was, as she had suspected, the type of man who took his amusement where he found 't, and he had anticipated she might be willing to accommodate him. He was disappointed to discover that she was virtuous.

He was looking absently at the scratch upon his hand.

'*C'était écrit,*' he murmured.

It was written, in other words, fated. She took him up on that.

'We do seem fated to meet in odd circumstances,' she said brightly.

'But fate can be circumvented,' he returned cryptically, and his mouth set in an obstinate line. 'My course is set and I refuse to be deflected from it.'

'Naturally, m'sieur.' She wondered what he was talking about.

He glanced up at her with a flicker of menace in his eyes.

'So no siren songs from you, *ma mie,* even though you are a water nymph.'

She flushed angrily. Did he still think she was avail-

47

able, or worse still suspect that she was attracted by him?

'I wouldn't waste any time on them, and I can't sing.'

He sprang to his feet with a sudden change of mood.

'*Mon Dieu*, what am I doing, delaying your return with foolish utterances—you are chilled and hurt and should be on your way home.' He looked anxiously at her pale face. 'I wish I had some cognac to give you.'

'Monsieur, I don't wish you to put yourself out further for me,' she said with cold dignity, for she did not trust him. 'I'll manage to get myself home.'

She rose to her feet and winced as her weight came upon her injured foot, as she reached for her sodden sandal.

'Sit down,' he commanded, and kicked the sandal away with quite unnecessary violence, then as she remained standing he put his hands upon her shoulders and forced her down on to the boulder. He stood in front of her, his fingers digging into her flesh, regarding her through half closed lids, with a slumbrous sensuous expression.

'You need no songs with those great eyes,' he murmured. 'Eyes like a forest pool, now green, now brown, in which a man could drown.' Abruptly he took his hands away, while Halcyon's heart beat a mad tattoo. 'You cannot hobble down to the village,' he went on with a change of tone and expression. 'And since Saracen is here, you can ride back.'

'Oh, monsieur, I hate having to put you to so much trouble.'

'*N'importe*. Will you promise not to move while I fetch my horse?'

'Is it really necessary?'

'Have you any other solution?' She shook her head. '*Eh bien*, do as you are told.'

48

He turned to go, then swung back to her.

'Wait, I have a better idea. I will take you to him.'

Before she realised his intention, he had picked her up in his arms. Carrying her with ease, he covered the short distance between them and the tethered horse, and put her sideways on the saddle. Then disengaging the reins from the tree, he gathered them in his left hand and setting his foot in the stirrup, sprang up behind her.

Saracen, resenting the double burden, started to curvet, and the man's arm closed round Halcyon's waist, holding her close against him.

'*Taisez-vous,*' he said to the horses. '*Alors, en avant!*'

The animal began to pick its way down the steep descent.

Halcyon's feelings were indescribable. The arm that enclosed her was like a steel band, pressing her against his muscular chest; the material of his shirt was against her cheek, it smelled of lavender and herbs. His chin was touching her hair, her legs lay across his knee. Every nerve in her body tingled at the enforced pressure, and though her predicament had brought about this situation, he had no need to hold her so close. Her pride forbade protest, nor did she think it would be of any avail. He would have some glib answer ready to justify his action and it was true the horse was skittish, a sufficient excuse, though she did not believe her security was his real motive. By her own carelessness she had given him this advantage and she could not complain about the consequences.

When they reached the main road, he urged Saracen to a trot, and his hold became even tighter, but when they reached the outskirts of the village, he stopped and dismounted. Taking hold of the bridle, he led the horse, while Halcyon changed her position to sit astride the saddle.

'You can ride, mademoiselle?' he asked, noticing her action.

'A little, cross-saddle.'

'Perhaps I could find you a mount.'

'That's very kind of you, but I wouldn't dream of putting you to so much trouble.'

If it was his intention to woo Mariette she wanted no more contact with him. At twenty-two one is very susceptible to a handsome face, without considering what lies beneath it. He was, she judged, some seven or eight years older than she was, and being French had no doubt sown some wild oats. His assurance had the seal of experience, and she knew instinctively that he could only bring her unhappiness.

'Why not?' he demanded.

'Monsieur, we're strangers.'

'Not since you have been in my arms.' He slanted an audacious look upwards to her. 'Our acquaintance has progressed by leaps and bounds, Mademoiselle Grey.'

Of course he would know her name, but she still was unsure of his.

'You know who I am, since I'm your tenant,' she told him, 'but I don't know your name—unless it is Monsieur de Valprès.' She looked at him enquiringly.

'Nowadays it is always first names among the young. Call me Raoul.'

'I couldn't.'

Again he asked: 'Why not?'

There was no answer to that except that she wished to avoid intimacy with him, but to tell him that would not be polite.

'Very well, Raoul,' she said without enthusiasm.

'And your first name?'

'Does it matter?' she parried.

'I wish to know it.' He was imperious.

Well, fair was fair, he had told her his.

'Halcyon,' she informed him, looking out between the horse's ears.

''Alcyone,' he repeated wonderingly. '*Eh bien, naturellement* it would not be Marie or Jeanne. It is suitable to a water nymph.'

'But you prefer pigeons,' she said, intending to needle him.

He laughed. 'It is not a question of préference, *chérie.*'

The merriment died out of his face and his expression hardened, as he fixed his eyes on the road ahead of them. Dimly Halcyon sensed some inner conflict was at war within him but had no idea what was causing it. In spite of what he had said, he was merely a chance acquaintance, and she had no clue to his personal problems which were not her concern anyway, nor had he any right to call her darling.

In spite of that she did not resent the endearment as she should have done, and her eyes were very soft as she looked down at the black head level with her knee. Whatever intentions he might have been harbouring towards her his conduct today could not have been more chivalrous.

They were passing along the village street, and several of its denizens stopped to gaze at them, astonished by the spectacle of a bare-legged girl astride a great horse, being led by a man they obviously knew, for the men touched their forelocks and the women nodded to him. There would be much speculation in the bistro tonight about the mad English girl and the local Casanova.

Raoul halted as they reached the cottage, and flung Saracen's reins over a post in the paling. Halcyon made a movement to dismount, but as she brought her leg over the saddle he forestalled her. She felt his firm hands on her waist as he lifted her down. He kept them there, as he said:

'You should not walk on that foot.'

'Oh, nonsense!'

'It is not nonsense,' he returned gravely, and again he lifted her. She had left the door unlocked in case her father returned in her absence, and he pushed it open, carrying her into the narrow passage. Felix called from the studio, indicating that he was home.

'Is that you, Hal? Where have you been?'

Raoul opened the door and went in, while Felix turned from his easel to regard them with astonishment.

'Hal, you've had an accident?'

A low couch stood underneath the skylight which Felix sometimes used to pose a model. Raoul deposited Halcyon upon it, as he explained:

'Mademoiselle Grey cut her foot. Fortunately I was passing and able to assist. I do not think the injury is serious.'

He turned towards the artist and his eyes fell upon the picture upon the easel. It was Felix's 'photograph' of the chateau to which he was putting the final touches before delivering it. Raoul gave it a quizzical look as he introduced himself, this time without any evasion.

'De Valprès,' Felix said musingly. 'There is no doubt where you originated, monsieur. I've seen your features reproduced far too many times during the past few weeks to be in any doubt about that.'

Raoul smiled wryly. 'I expect you have, Monsieur Grey. The de Valprès run true to type even after a period in Canada, whither they went after the Revolution.'

Deeply interested, Halcyon asked: 'But didn't I hear you say the last of the name died on the guillotine?'

'I said the last Comtesse. We dropped the title in Canada. Her husband and son escaped, they were in hiding when the chateau was attacked, they did not believe the *sans-culottes* would war upon women. When they discovered Antoinette was dead they managed to get to England and afterwards emigrated. It was not our own people who rose against the chateau, but the soldiers of the *commune*. Our peasants were loyal, but we had never oppressed them like the majority of our peers. They loved Antoinette, who was very good to them. It was they who planted the first of the willow trees in her memory.'

'A nice thought,' Felix commented. 'When I'm free of my commitments, I should like to paint those weeping willows. They are very lovely.'

'You should put your daughter into the picture,' Raoul suggested, 'and call it The Naiad—water nymph.'

'That's an idea.' Felix became enthusiastic.

Both men regarded Halcyon lying gracefully on the couch, bathed in the cold white light from the skylight above her, her skimpy green dress outlining her figure, and her hair spread about her neck and shoulders.

'Reclining like that,' Felix said, screwing up his eyes, 'with her hair loose and without her dress.'

Raoul grinned delightedly. 'I shall look forward to seeing that picture, though I have already seen her without her clothes.'

Felix gave him a keen glance, while Halcyon blushed furiously.

'You don't mean in the nude?' he said frostily.

'I had my swimsuit on,' Halcyon interposed.

'You were swimming in the pool?' Felix was eyeing Raoul suspiciously. 'I thought you were always alone.'

Raoul said imperturbably, 'We met by accident under your willow trees. She was charming, and I am sure she would be a much more congenial task to paint than cleaning my ancestor's saturnine features.'

'Doesn't it irk you to have them in Dubois' possession?' Felix asked bluntly, thinking that even if Raoul did not have the means to acquire the chateau he could have made an offer for the pictures.

Raoul shrugged his shoulders. 'They belong there, it would be a shame to transplant them.' His face darkened and he seemed to forget his audience. 'It is I who must join them.'

Felix raised his brows with a little knowing smile, while Halcyon felt suddenly cold. They both knew what was in Raoul's mind, but he did not seem very elated by the prospect. She relaxed on the hard couch, feeling utterly weary as her interest in Raoul's story faded. Outside, Saracen stamped and whinnied, and the Frenchman came out of his reverie as his glance fell upon Halcyon's white face.

'*Mon Dieu*, but we are neglectful!' he exclaimed. ''Alcyone needs a drink and to bathe her wound while we stand chattering about inessentials.'

Felix went to a cupboard in the wall. 'A sip of brandy, Hal, there's a drop left.'

'No, thank you, Daddy, but I'd love a cup of tea.'

'I'll make one. A pity Louis isn't here. He could be useful for once.' Felix disliked domestic chores.

'Louis?' Raoul's voice was sharp as a whipcrack and his black brows rose enquiringly.

'An artist friend of my father's,' Halcyon said

54

quickly, adding mischievously, for she knew how he regarded the beverage, 'Won't you join us for a cup?'

'*Merci*, but I must be on my way before Saracen removes your palings.' Raoul moved towards the door. 'Take good care of that foot, 'Alcyone, *au revoir*. *Adieu*, Monsieur Grey.'

Felix went to make the tea and Halcyon lay listening to Saracen's retreating hooves. Then she remembered that Raoul's handkerchief was still about her foot. She must wash it and somehow return it to him. She did not know where he lived, but Monsieur Blum could tell her. The prospect of this small service was oddly comforting, it indicated there was still a link between them.

Felix returned with the tea things upon a tray and poured out a cup for her.

'Don't you become any further involved with Monsieur le Comte,' he said warningly. 'He has other fish to fry, my girl, and though he may have repudiated the title, unless I'm much mistaken in him, he's not above claiming the privileges of his station.'

Halcyon smiled wanly. '*Le droit du seigneur?*' she asked. 'Come off it, Daddy, we live in modern times.'

'Which are not so unlike the former days, with this vaunted permissiveness,' he said heavily, with his eyes on the porcelain delicacy of his daughter's features. For the first time he felt she was his responsibility.

Halcyon sipped the welcome tea. 'We're unlikely to see him again,' she pointed out. 'And we're not his vassals.' She set down her cup. 'Now I really must do something about my foot. Could you get a bowl of warm water and some plaster?'

'You haven't told me how it happened yet,' her father complained.

'I will when you come back, it was quite an adventure.' She laughed a little forcedly.

Felix departed not very willingly upon this errand, he was more used to being waited upon by others than ministering to them.

When he had gone, Halcyon remembered with a slight sense of shock that though they were not his vassals, she had discovered they were Raoul de Valprès' tenants. The roof and walls that sheltered them were his property, and as they were on a weekly tenancy, he could if he so desired turn them out.

CHAPTER FOUR

CONFINED to the house next morning, for her foot was unpleasantly painful, Halcyon sought distraction with her pen. Since Felix was absent, she opened the shutters of the studio window to admit the sunlight, but inspiration would not flow. Since meeting Raoul by the Roman bath, her own life had all the ingredients of a novelette, culminating in the mishap of her wounded foot and that ride down the valley, with Raoul, Mariette and herself comprising the eternal triangle. But in her story she could manipulate the characters as she chose, so long as she ensured a happy ending. In reality such incidents were unconnected. She was unlikely to meet Raoul again; he was, she was fairly certain, contemplating a marriage of convenience with Mariette, and her own part in their lives was negligible. If she cast herself as the heroine there could be no happy ending, no ending at all in fact, but merely a fade-out.

Her pen slid from her fingers as she gave up the attempt to rough out a plot on the pad she was holding, for she never composed straight on to a typewriter. She had intended her hero to be a Nordic giant, but Raoul's dark Latin face came between her and her original conception. As for her heroine, could any flesh and blood girl be quite so inane, so ready to misunderstand as the woman she was trying to create? But she was no more silly than herself, who could not get

Raoul out of her mind, when he was obviously set upon a course that would lead him far away from her.

Felix came home for lunch in a bad humour. The Dubois girl, he told her, was a tiresome model, she could not hold a pose for more than a couple of minutes and she talked incessantly.

'Her face is completely empty,' he grumbled. 'All I can make of her is the sort of pictures you used to find on a box of chocolates.'

'Which is all Papa wants,' Halcyon consoled him. 'So long as you make her look pretty, he won't care how insipid she looks and will be perfectly satisfied.' She glanced at her watch. 'But you're back early.'

'They wanted me out of the way. Madame de Valprès is coming to lunch. She and her son live in the vicinity, as we surmised. You'd think she was royalty, they only stopped short of laying out a red carpet. Moreover, they continually refer to her as Madame la Comtesse, though the son gave us to understand they'd given up the title.'

'So they have, titles are an anachronism in republican France.'

'Then I bet Dubois will try to revive it. That's why he's so keen on the proposed match. Your cavalier of yesterday, my girl, is the reigning Comte, since his mother is a widow—the Dubois had all the facts at their fingers' ends. I didn't know we had such distinguished neighbours.'

'We've never bothered to know any of our neighbours.'

'We haven't had time. I'm told de Valprès owns a farm and a prosperous vineyard, and I could see from his dress and horse he wasn't exactly a pauper.'

'I hope you didn't relate yesterday's incident to Mademoiselle Dubois?' Halcyon asked anxiously. 'She might not have been ... amused.'

'What do you take me for?' Felix growled. 'I have some discretion. It's obvious what's brewing, though personally I wouldn't take on that empty-headed little chatterbox for all the chateaux along the Loire.'

'She's only a means to an end,' Halcyon said a little bitterly. 'Frenchmen expect a dowry with their brides, don't they?'

'They did, I don't know about the present generation, but since the de Valprès are *ancien régime* they certainly will. I expect this marvellous ball Mariette enthuses about will celebrate more than her birthday.'

Halcyon sighed involuntarily. 'You think Madame de Valprès has gone to discuss ... terms?'

Felix shrugged his shoulders. 'Probably, but I neither know nor care. We don't belong to their world.'

He started to unpack the bag containing his painting gear, which he had brought back with him, while Halcyon doodled aimlessly on her pad. Her father's words had been a timely reminder. The de Valprès were people who moved in a different sphere from impecunious artists.

A tap on the unshuttered window startled them both, and they were surprised to see one of the people they had been discussing looking in.

Felix pushed open the half closed window.

'Your servant, Monsieur le Comte,' he said mockingly.

Raoul frowned. 'That is all finished with,' he said coldly.

'The Dubois don't seem to think so. I spent the morning at the Chateau until I was turned out when Madame de Valprès was expected. She is lunching there, as I expect you know.'

Felix's face wore a sly look, but Raoul's was completely expressionless.

'*Tant pis*,' he said coolly. His eyes sought Halcyon and he smiled at her. 'I called to enquire about the wounded foot.'

'It's nothing much,' she assured him, 'only a little sore when I try to walk. Daddy, let Monsieur de Valprès in.'

'Do not disarrange yourself,' Raoul bade him. He leaned negligently against the window frame. 'I cannot stop, much as I should like to do so.' His eyes lingered upon Halcyon.

'You also are bound for the chateau?' Felix enquired.

'Not this time.'

Halcyon moved restlessly under his unwavering gaze. She was wearing a clean white dress with her hair loose about her shoulders, and again no stockings. She had not expected anyone to call, except perhaps Louis, and he was so familiar he hardly counted. Self-consciously she gathered up her hair into a knot behind her head.

'Please excuse my untidiness, I wasn't expecting visitors.'

'But surely you knew I would call to enquire about the foot?' Raoul said reproachfully.

'No, monsieur. It's only a trivial cut, unworthy of your concern.'

Felix looked from one to the other with amusement. His daughter's distrait manner was not lost upon him, nor the admiration in the young man's glance.

'You'd better change your mind and come in and have a drink,' he invited. 'I've got something better than tea to offer you.'

Halcyon raised her eyebrows as he produced a bottle out of his bag. Felix had been extravagant. It occurred to her that unlike herself he had expected this call.

'Monsieur Grey, you are most amiable,' Raoul declared. '*Permettez-moi.*' He climbed agilely over the low window sill.

Standing beside Felix, Halcyon saw he was taller than her father and broader in the shoulder, exuding a dark magnetism that reduced the artist to a pale shadow. He dangled his riding crop from the fingers of one hand.

'You're riding?' she asked, while Felix went to the cupboard for glasses.

'Saracen needs exercise. I hope your paling is stout if he becomes impatient, but I could not resist your father's invitation.'

So for the second time the black horse was tied to their fence. Halcyon wondered with inward amusement what the villagers would make of it. Too bad if the gossip got round to Mariette.

Felix held up the bottle.

'You probably know this, de Valprès?'

Raoul nodded and laughed. 'I should do. We made it.'

Felix poured out three glasses full and handed one to him and another to his daughter.

'That was a good vintage year,' Raoul told them, holding his glass up to the light. '*Santé.*' He gave Halcyon a mischievous look. 'So you do drink other things besides tea?'

'Upon occasion,' she returned demurely.

'And this is an occasion?'

'We don't often have such august company, monsieur.'

'*Quelle sotise!*' He snapped his fingers. 'And my name is Raoul.'

He stood between Halcyon and the window, a debonair vibrant figure in his riding gear. Her eyes became big and soft—she could not help it, was unaware of it, he was so very good to look at. He caught her glance and smiled very sweetly. Hastily she looked away.

Felix raised his brows, catching the exchange, and swept some papers off a chair.

'Take a seat, de Valprès.'

Raoul deliberately moved the chair with his foot nearer to Halcyon before he sat down.

'You must come and see the vines that produce this,' he told her.

'I'm sure it would be an interesting expedition,' Felix observed, 'but it's a long way, isn't it, and we've no transport.'

Raoul's eyes glinted mockingly.

'But 'Alcyone is a good walker.'

'Not at present,' she said firmly, 'nor for some time to come.' She had no intention of traipsing over the countryside to view Raoul's home—besides, whatever would his mother think?

'I could send the car.'

'Thank you very much, but we're busy people,' she told him quickly. She looked at him meaningfully. 'We won't waste your time and ours.'

His eyes met hers in a long look, and to her annoyance she felt her colour rise.

'It might not be a waste of time,' he said softly.

Halcyon turned her head away. That slumbrous, sensuous regard of his always disturbed her, and she had an uneasy suspicion that he knew it. He was trying to flirt with her, which since he was half engaged to Mariette Dubois, was reprehensible. Gaining no response from her, he looked round the room critically and noticed the oil lamp on its bracket.

'I am thinking of having electricity installed here,' he announced. 'You would find it a convenience, yes? I shall give Blum the necessary instructions.'

'We ... we don't miss it, she faltered.

Felix broke in. 'Oh, but we do. It would make life a lot easier, I'm sure.'

'And the plumbing could possibly do with some improvement?'

Felix laughed. 'I'd say it could.'

'We may not be staying here much longer ...' Halcyon began, not wishing to be under an obligation to him.

'We've made no other plans,' Felix interrupted.

Raoul stood up.

'I hope you will stay for a long time, Monsieur Grey, and in any case I ought to keep my property up to date. Blum should have advised me that the arrangements here were primitive. It shall be seen to. And now, since Saracen grows impatient,' they could hear the beast stamping and snorting, 'I must be on my way.' He bowed formally to Halcyon, bidding her adieu, and Felix went with him to the door. He came back chuckling.

'What it is to have a pretty daughter! I bet our landlord wouldn't have concerned himself with electricity and plumbing if he hadn't met you.'

'He'll double the rent,' she said tartly.

'If he does we can afford it with what we're making out of Monsieur Dubois, but I don't think he will. It would spoil the gesture.' His face became serious. 'Not smitten, are you, Hal?'

'Oh, no,' she exclaimed, and went on to elaborate, as much to convince herself as her father. 'I don't care for that romantic, Latin type, too theatrical, and in any case I've more sense than to fall for a philanderer, as he obviously is, apart from his involvement with Mariette.'

Felix's face cleared, as he gave a sigh of relief.

'I'm glad you've got him taped,' he observed, and went to close the shutters prior to starting work.

Raoul was as good as his word. Monsieur Blum arrived with electricians, and surveyors to plan the improvements. A water heater was to be fitted over the stone sink, an annexe built on to the kitchen to house a closet and a shower. An electric cooker would replace the oil stove. As soon as the estimates were approved the work would be begun. The de Valprès seemed able to obviate the usual delays. Monsieur Blum warned the Greys that naturally the rent would be increased with these amenities, an eventuality that Halcyon had foreseen. For that reason she did not welcome the innovations. In summer weather the drawback to the cottage, the outdoor sanitation, and primitive lighting and heating, were no great imposition, and she was anxious to build up Felix's bank balance, so that Raoul's good intentions were from her point of view misplaced.

Raoul came to see them a few days later, this time driving his car, a long black Mercedes-Benz. Seeing this sign of affluence, Halcyon reflected that whatever regrets he had for the chateau, his vineyards must be flourishing.

She experienced the familiar quickening of her pulses as she heard Raoul's voice outside. He was accompanied by Monsieur Blum and they were discussing the dimensions of the new annexe. Though they were speaking in French, she knew enough to understand the gist of what they were saying, and their voices floated in to her through the open kitchen window. Monsieur Blum declared:

'It will be a fairly expensive business, but you will in time recover your outlay by an increase in rent. What would you suggest would be a fair charge?'

'There will be no increase,' Raoul told him decisively. 'You have been charging too much for this shack in the state it was. If anything you owe Monsieur Grey a rebate.'

The agent began to expostulate, but Raoul took no notice. He came to rap on the back door.

'*Quelqu'un chez soi?*'

Halcyon went to the door. She had been cooking their evening meal, enveloped in a print overall, her hair tied back by a ribbon. She seemed fated to encounter Raoul looking her worst. Because of that, she said coldly:

'Yes, Monsieur de Valprès?'

Today he wore a formal suit, charcoal grey with snowy linen, and she wondered if he had been to the chateau.

'You have heard what we propose to do?' he asked. 'I hope that will meet with your requirements?'

'I was quite content with the place as it was,' she said ungraciously, noticing that Monsieur Blum was looking at her with a knowing eye. His frugal French soul had been shocked by Raoul's refusal to raise the rent, but now a new idea had occurred to him and Halcyon guessed what was passing in his mind. Something of the sort had also been in hers, and she added: 'I don't see why you should put yourself to so much trouble and expense for us. Eventually we'll be moving on.'

'I hope to make Le Nid so comfortable that you will be unable to bear to leave it,' he told her blandly, ignoring his agent's avid ears.

65

'Very thoughtful of you,' she said vaguely, not knowing quite what to say to that.

'Gracedieu is honoured by the presence of a famous artist,' he stated airily, as if that accounted for his interest in them.

'Not so very famous. Will you come in?'

He shook his head. 'I am on my way to the chateau.' So he was going not coming from it. 'This time I go by invitation.'

If Monsieur Blum had not been there she would have been tempted to ask if he had changed his mind about the *parvenu* Dubois, since he was ready to fraternise with them after calling them usurpers, but she could answer her own question. Madame la Mère had pointed out the value of an alliance with the upstart daughter and he was about to commence his courtship.

'Well, that's a nice change from the time I met you,' she said brightly, and to her surprise he scowled. 'I won't keep you. And thank you for all you're doing for us.'

Monsieur Blum said something that she did not catch, and Raoul explained:

'We are afraid you may suffer some inconvenience while the alterations are being made. I must see if I can make some arrangement for you.'

'Oh, please don't bother, we'll manage,' she told him quickly. 'Daddy would hate to leave his studio and that won't be much disturbed. The electricians could put the light fittings in while he was at the chateau.'

'Ah, yes, the chateau,' he exclaimed as if some idea had occurred to him.

Though he had refused to come in, he seemed disposed to linger, though his agent was fidgeting impatiently. A smell from the oil oven claimed Halcyon's attention.

66

'You must excuse me, monsieur, my cooking is burning.'

To her dismay he followed her into the kitchen, as she hastened to take a pudding out of the oven. It was a simple confection, sponge over fruit, and it came out nicely browned.

'That looks most appetising,' he observed as she put it on the table. 'You are an accomplished woman, 'Alcyone.'

'Most women can cook,' she said, flushing, for he was standing almost touching her and his proximity made her nervous. 'I couldn't compare with your French chefs.'

'They do not make puddings,' he informed her. 'That is an item of English cuisine. When I was in England, and I have been in England, I was particularly partial to ... what do you call it? Jam roly-poly. Can you make that?'

'Usually, sometimes the jam runs out.'

'Perhaps one day you will make one for me and the jam will not run out.'

'With pleasure, Monsieur de Valprès. We'll ask you to dinner when the new cooker has been installed.'

'That is a promise? But why so formal? I was to be Raoul, was I not?'

She glanced at the open door, through which she could see the agent lingering. Raoul followed the direction of her gaze, and added, 'When we are *en famille*.'

'Which we aren't at this moment. You'll be late for your visit, won't you?'

He shrugged his shoulders. '*N'importe*. But your father will be wanting his dinner.' Felix was shut in his studio, deeply engrossed and as usual unaware of anything that was happening around him.

Raoul raised his hand and lightly touched her cheek. '*Au 'voir, chérie.*'

'Goodbye, Raoul.' She spoke his name very softly so that Blum could not hear.

He smiled at the use of his name and sauntered out of the back door. Halcyon watched him go, her finger to the cheek that he had touched. She heard him speak to the agent, and saw them pass the window, then the sound of Raoul's car as he turned on the ignition.

Again he had called her *chérie*, it was not a word that should be spoken by another woman's suitor. What was coming to life between herself and Raoul must be sternly checked. That there was something could not be denied, but she must not let herself yield to it. Pride alone would not permit her to play the other woman in their triangle. Raoul would see no harm in dallying with the poverty-stricken artist's daughter, might even believe that she was ripe for a little amorous diversion, but she was not that sort of girl, she had too much self-respect, even if she had no dowry. The sooner Raoul's betrothal to Mariette was announced the better, for then she would have a concrete weapon to use against him.

She spread the check tablecloth on the table, the cutlery glasses for the *vin ordinaire* and the bread. Then she turned her attention to the *bouillon* she had cooked, as she heard her father close his studio door, reflecting that it would be as well if Raoul forgot about his roly-poly.

He must have mentioned to the Dubois the inconvenience to which they were shortly to be exposed, for Felix came back next day with an invitation to stay at the chateau while the alterations were being done.

'Monsieur assures me that he has plenty of room,' he said, his eyes twinkling. 'There are only about twenty

68

bedrooms in that mausoleum. Also he believes the portrait will progress more quickly if I'm on the spot. You'll remember Mariette suggested it herself.'

'I also remember she did not include me.'

'Oh, she's become quite keen to have you. We've impressed upon her that you're an authority upon historical period dress and will be able to help her with her costume for this *bal masqué*. Since they've chosen to represent the Empire, she fancies herself as Pauline Bonaparte who was reputed to be a beauty, while Papa will disport himself as Napoleon. I only hope Mama has no aspirations towards Josephine, who was famed for her elegance. She's dumpier than her daughter.'

'I don't want to go,' Halcyon told him bluntly.

'It won't be for long, and they can get the work done much more quickly if we're not here to get in the way.'

'We shouldn't be in the way. At least, not much.'

Felix looked a little dashed. 'I'm sorry you're so against it. I thought you'd enjoy a chance to stay in a genuine chateau, but I'm afraid your objections come too late—I've accepted. We're to have a whole tower to ourselves, and it'll be much pleasanter than falling over plumbers and electricians.'

Under any other circumstances, Halcyon would have welcomed a chance to stay in such a place and the preparations for the ball promised to be fun. She did know quite a lot about historical costumes, and had been researching the Napoleonic era for the background to her novel. But to be in daily contact with Raoul's future wife, to have to listen, as she was sure she would, to talk not only about the dance, but the impending engagement, would be something of an ordeal, it might even be painful. She was uncertain of

69

the state of her feelings towards Raoul, but the little prick of jealousy she experienced whenever his marriage to Mariette was mentioned warned her that she was not indifferent.

Upon reflection, she decided that for that reason the visit would be also salutary for her and dissipate the romantic dreams she was beginning to cherish about Raoul de Valprès. If the invitation had been prompted by him it illustrated how little he was interested in her, for if he were, he would not want her at the chateau. He had been concerned about their comfort, which showed a natural kindliness, and thought she might be of assistance to Mariette, but he had no personal feeling for herself beyond a superficial gallantry, which was probably his normal approach to a pretty girl.

So she withdrew her opposition and began to make sketches of Empire costumes which might appeal to the Dubois, neglecting her novel to do so. Residence at the chateau might provide the stimulus she needed to continue with it, which at the moment was entirely lacking.

Dubois gave them what amounted to a suite, the top floor of one of the two towers. There was a spacious sitting room between the two bedrooms where Felix could house his easel and she her typewriter. It also had its own bathroom. Plumbing had been installed where necessary by its new owner, though it had not lacked in this respect, since during the war the chateau had been used as a hospital. There were various powder closets and *garde-robes* which had been utilised for this purpose. Their windows offered them fine views, over the river upon one side, and overlooking the Roman bath on the other. From her bedroom Halcyon could look down upon the rounded feathery tops of the weeping willows, and recall, as she frequently did, her first meeting with Raoul.

Felix was intent upon finishing Mariette's portrait as quickly as possible, so that he could go on to more congenial work. Her sittings were irregular and erratic, but he was able to do a good deal without her, painting diligently both morning and afternoon. The background comprised a draped curtain, and that hung in the studio, drawn aside to disclose a glimpse of the chateau in the distance, at Papa's special request. When Mariette did condescend to appear, Halcyon absented herself, for her presence distracted the girl even more. She either retired to her own room or went for a walk.

The twin towers were linked by the main apartments, which were much bigger rooms, and in them the family was located. The Greys' meals were brought up to them, and only by special invitation did they dine with their hosts, an arrangement that both Felix and his daughter infinitely preferred to having to make conversation with Papa and Mama Dubois.

More and more frequently as time went on, Mariette would send her maid to request Halcyon to join her in her luxurious bedroom, to discuss her costume for the ball, which was being made by a local dressmaker, and also the decorations for the ballroom, which was in fact the great central hall of the chateau, in which a special floor was being laid for the event. She also insisted that her guest accompanied her upon shopping expeditions, and they drove as far afield as Orléans in search of designs and pictures. Halcyon suggested that as it was a military epoch, the hall should be decked with regimental standards, and that meant hunting up the ensigns borne by the troops of Napoleon's armies. Mariette was pleasant and

71

friendly, deferring to the other girl's greater knowledge.

'For I wish all to be *comme il faut*,' she declared.

She was woefully ignorant of history and it was only through having read a light romance about them that she had even heard of Napoleon's sisters. She changed from Pauline to Caroline Murat when she learned that the latter had been Queen of Naples, and her husband, Joachim Murat, was the most dashing of her brother's officers.

'And Raoul must be Joachim,' she announced, and giggled. 'It will only be anticipating a little.'

She did not often mention Raoul, and whenever she had occasion to do so, she would look at Halcyon a little maliciously, from which Halcyon deduced she had heard some gossip about them. She was certain he visited the chateau frequently, but Mariette always took care she was out of the way when he appeared.

Caroline was a happy choice for Mademoiselle Dubois, for she appeared to have been small and plump, and being Corsican she should have been dark, though some authorities claim she was fair.

'Like nowadays,' Mariette commented. 'One can be blonde or brunette according to one's fancy.'

Being a queen she would be able to wear a diamond tiara, which was why Mariette had chosen the character.

There was only one moment of friction. The Greys had been invited to dine with the Dubois, and Mariette was holding forth about her costume, when her father asked:

'And who will Mademoiselle Grey personify?'

'I have not asked her,' Mariette said carelessly.

'Do you mean you do not know who she is going to represent, or that you have not asked her to the ball?'

Mariette looked sullen. 'It is for friends and relatives.'

'Are not the Greys our good friends?' He turned to his wife. 'Mama, did you not give them a card?'

Madame Dubois looked unhappily at Mariette. 'It was not necessary since they are staying in the chateau,' she mumbled.

Pierre Dubois gave each of his womenfolk a sharp glance, then said:

'*Ma foi*, but of course you are both invited. Forgive the oversight.'

'I really don't mind about it ...' Halcyon began.

Dubois became incensed. 'Mind? *Ciel, naturellement* you must mind. To be excluded from such a pageant, the event of the century! You would be *désolée*. I am hoping that it will inspire *Monsieur votre père* to a picture.' Felix made a grimace, which he hastily concealed with his table napkin. 'What will you go as, monsieur?'

'Just an artist. They had painters even during that martial age.'

'Just so.' Dubois looked a little puzzled as he tried to remember who had been famous during that period.

'I believe Madame Vigée-Lebrun was still existent,' Halcyon said, anxious to appease him. 'In fact I think she painted one of the Bonapartes. That would be a nice simple costume.' She looked placatingly at Mariette.

'But yes, that would do well for you,' Mariette agreed more amiably, since she saw no danger of being outshone.

Halcyon had been quite reconciled to her non-appearance, for she had expected neither she nor her father would be asked, since they did not belong to the

Dubois' circle. She had meant to watch the proceedings from some hidden corner and she was not altogether pleased at her inclusion. She would not know anybody and it would only mean being a visible wallflower instead of an invisible spectator, besides which she would have to waste time and thought upon making up a dress for herself.

She abandoned the idea of representing any known character, being unable to find a picture of Madame Lebrun at the age she must have reached during the Empire. Madame Camplan occurred to her as suitable, for that famous schoolmistress would fit her mood, but she would not be recognisable. Finally she decided she would simply be a lady of the period. In that she was helped by an unexpectedly generous gift from Mariette, who offered her a length of white muslin, which she had bought and then rejected as not sumptuous enough for her own adornment. Her gown was to be of silk, heavily embroidered with gold. Possibly her kindness was tempered by the thought that Halcyon would appear nondescript in such simple material, but Halcyon gave her the benefit of the doubt. Without being a skilled needlewoman, she was able to run up a plain gown, falling in straight lines from the high waist. It had a square neckline and puffed sleeves.

I look like a little girl dressed for a party, she thought, when she surveyed herself in her mirror, the effect heightened by a broad blue sash. She did not notice how becoming to her long-legged figure were the soft folds falling to her feet, but she did remember that ladies of that period used to dampen their dresses to make them cling, though her love of historical accuracy would not extend to that length.

The midsummer days sped past, while the preparations gathered momentum. The alterations to Le Nid were also well under way. Halcyon hoped that they would be able to move back again after the ball was over. She had had enough of being sequestered like the Lady of Shalott in her tower.

At length the great day dawned. Guests poured in from all over the countryside and from faraway Paris. Some were to stay overnight at the chateau, others had found accommodation in nearby villages. Halcyon had suggested that she and her father should move out to make more room, but Dubois would not hear of it. He had an idea that if Felix left, the portrait, now nearing completion, would never be finished, and Mariette surprisingly added her protests to her father's. Only Halcyon knew how to dress her in her regalia for the ball.

'In any case we have too many people staying for the night,' she declared. 'Maman says the servants will go ... what you say ... on strike if we have any more.'

But something seemed to have gone awry for the daughter of the Chateau, for several days before the ball she was out of temper, but she did not confide to Halcyon the cause of her grievance, though she muttered occasional complaints about the selfishness of men. Halcyon wondered if Raoul had managed to displease her, but did not think that was probable upon the eve of their engagement. Both he and his mother were to be present, that fact was circulated proudly among the Dubois' bourgeois guests.

On the momentous evening, Halcyon had to be present at Mariette's 'robing' although she also had in attendance her maid, a hairdresser and the dressmaker. Flatteringly she asked her opinion upon each stage of her toilet. Was her hair in the correct style? Would it be correct to wear a scarf? Were patches in order? Etc, etc.

75

When she was finished, she was gorgeous to behold. Her silk dress clung to her rounded hips stiff with gold embroidery that, heavy at the hem, thinned out in a spiralling pattern nearly as far as her high waist. A diamond pendant, her father's birthday present, encircled her throat, and the diamond tiara glittered in her dark hair, from which at Halcyon's suggestion, one ringlet fell upon her bared shoulder, which the deep circular line of her bodice revealed. A filmy stole of gold net hung from her arms in the style dictated by Halcyon, who told her it must not be drawn over her shoulders. A jewelled belt enclosed her waist, which the fashion of that day necessitated being almost as high as her armpits, a fashion that was kind to her, making her short legs look longer than they were. Finally she put on long gloves reaching to above her elbows.

'I cannot wear rings with these,' she observed.

'No,' Halcyon agreed.

'But should it be necessary to put one on,' she gave the other girl an arch look, 'I could perhaps take them off?'

'Of course,' Halcyon said steadily. Mariette was hoping before the evening was over to be wearing Raoul's ring.

Mariette pirouetted in front of her long glass.

'Do I in truth look like a queen?' was her next question.

'Most regal, Your Majesty.' Halcyon made a mock curtsey.

Mariette gave a long sigh of satisfaction.

'I think myself it is *très chic*. I shall be the cynosure of all eyes and he ... he will regret that he did not do as I asked.'

An intriguing remark, but Halcyon had no idea to

whom she referred. If she were expecting Raoul to propose, he could not have offended her.

Reluctantly Mariette put on her mask, which was a mere strip of white velvet.

'Which I shall be happy to discard at midnight,' she declared.

She went off to show herself to her parents and Halcyon hurried away to her tower. Thanks to her preoccupation with Mariette, she had little time for her own toilet, but it was not elaborate. Like Mariette she dressed her hair high with a curl falling to one shoulder. Unlike Mariette she had no jewels to exhibit, only a gold locket and chain which had been her mother's. Felix refused to wait for her, saying he wanted to see the sycophants paying homage to the chateau's owners as they came in. He was wearing an artist's blouse and beret which he declared were suitable to any period. Halcyon did not think so, but she forbore to criticise. Felix wanted to be comfortable and he intended to latch himself on to the bar for most of the evening, where he would find some local acquaintances. He considered his daughter was capable of looking after herself.

Halcyon did not mind missing the beginning, she was in fact extremely reluctant to go downstairs at all. Although nothing had been actually said, there was an atmosphere of expectancy throughout the building, from its master to its humblest servant. Everyone was anticipating that the evening would culminate in the announcement of Raoul's engagement to Mariette Dubois. Many of the servants were drawn from the village and in spite of the republican era, had a lingering nostalgia for the old Comtes. Antoinette, in whose memory the willows were cultivated, had acquired the status of a legend. She had been so beautiful, so gener-

77

ous and so kind, she could never have been an enemy of the people; her execution had been a miscarriage of justice.

Everyone would be pleased to see her descendant back at the Chateau des Saules, where he rightly belonged, and it was fortuitous that Dubois had an only daughter, who could reinstate him.

Halcyon knew all this, and was inwardly shrinking from the spectacle of Mariette's triumph. She decided that she would not stay to witness it. Nobody, she felt sure, would notice if she were present or not, but she must put in an appearance, for if she did not, she might be confronted with awkward questions next day, and she did not wish to offend her kind host. She would stay for a little while in some secluded corner. At the same time, she was curious to see Raoul in the magnificent costume that she had helped to design for Murat. He would look wonderful, and only he could carry it off effectively. The King and Queen of Naples would be a glittering pair.

She could not face making an entrance down the grand stairway that led to the hall, but there were two flights up to the tower, one which connected with the main one, and another spiral stair which was seldom used. That had access to the hall through an unobtrusive door in the wall so that she could slip through without remark. So with a little sigh, she picked up the small fan with which she had provided herself, adjusted her mask, and made the twisty descent to the ballroom.

CHAPTER FIVE

THE great hall of the Chateau des Saules was rectangular in shape and occupied the centre of the building, its frontage contained the main entrance and terminated in each corner with one of the twin towers. Opposite the front door, a flight of shallow steps extended its full length, divided in the centre by the staircase, which ascended to a considerable height before branching off to left and right. The space on either side of it thus formed two daises, and on the night of the ball, one was assigned to the musicians, the other to the V.I.P.s.

Madame and Monsieur Dubois had finished receiving by the time Halcyon arrived and had retired to their seats on the dais, where they sat in a sort of regal state with their most important guests. Along each side of the hall was an arcade of pillars at a distance of some six feet from the walls. Flowers had been banked between them so that the space behind them formed secluded nooks for those who would rather observe than be observed. Groups of flags were fastened to project from each pillar, their blazonry bringing a bright note of colour to the grey stone. Bunting was strung across the hall linking the two arcades. Rows of small gilt chairs had been placed in front of the banks of flowers, for those who wished to advertise their desire to dance, but in the passage behind them was more comfortable seating for those who wanted to sit out.

Halcyon slipped like a little white ghost through the narrow doorway at the base of the tower. It was concealed by a stand of potted plants, so her entrance was as she had hoped unremarked. She had been in on the discussion when the decorations were planned, so she knew the layout, and turning aside behind the pillars, she walked behind them until she found a seat where the barricade of flowers and potted plants was low enough to permit her a limited view of the floor. There in the shadows she sat down and looked about her. By leaning forward she could obtain a sight of the dais. Madame Dubois wore purple velvet with diamond clasps from neck to hem of her Empire-style gown. Beside her was Madame de Valprès—at least Halcyon decided it must be she, in a dress of black velvet trimmed with silver, and she looked very much more at home amid the splendour about her than her poor hostess who was perspiring visibly with heat and anxiety. Halcyon studied her curiously, trying to discover a likeness to Raoul, but except that she was dark, there was little resemblance, except when she smiled. Raoul was a typical de Valprès, from whom he inherited his strange eyes. Hers appeared to be dark, and her hair was streaked with grey, while her features had the clear-cut outline of a cameo. A silver lamé stole covered her shoulders, not being worn in the correct period style over her arms which Halcyon had impressed upon Mariette. She was very much the aristocrat and made the dumpy Madame Dubois look plebeian. Pierre Dubois was standing behind them, self-conscious in his Napoleon's uniform. None of the three were masked.

Halcyon sat back and watched the dancers, who presented a gay kaleidoscope of colour. They were waltzing to Strauss, Monsieur Dubois having indicated very firmly that he would not tolerate any modern gymnastics tonight, and certainly their costumes were unsuitable to such antics. Most of the men wore military uniforms, there were hussars, cuirassiers, bemedalled generals and even a few infantrymen, and many of the chairs were occupied by the shakoes and helmets they had discarded while dancing. Halcyon saw with amusement one young man trip over the sword he had unwisely added to his dress and heard him swear beneath his breath. But apart from that trivial incident most of them wore their unfamiliar clothes with aplomb and re-created as Dubois had hoped they might the glory and glamour of the first Empire, before the snows of Russia had decimated Napoleon's Grand Armée. Halcyon felt a little glow of pride, for she had made a small contribution to this brilliant scene, and Dubois, from the smug satisfaction upon his rubicund face, was more than satisfied with its success.

It was not long before she discerned the Queen of Naples, there was no mistaking the gleam of her diamonds, but ... Halcyon rubbed her eyes ... the man she was dancing with wore the uniform that had been designed for Murat. Halcyon had seen the sketch for it, the tight breeches and polished boots and heavily gold-frogged tunic, that she recognised instantly, it was outstanding. A black velvet mask obscured the upper part of his face and he was dark-haired, but ... A mass of azaleas cut him off from her sight, and she waited eagerly for his next appearance. When the couple came again within her range of vision, she knew she was not mistaken. Mariette's partner was neither as tall nor as slim as Raoul, nor did he move with the same lithe grace. De Valprès must have refused to appear as Joachim Murat, and as the costume looked exceedingly uncomfortable, Halcyon could not blame him. That then explained Mariette's discontent and her complaint that he had refused to do as she requested. It was more than an objection to a flamboyant uniform. Mariette had attached significance to their appearance together as a married couple, the King and Queen of Naples, and Raoul's obstinacy had destroyed her pretty conceit. No wonder she had been annoyed and was bestowing her favours upon someone who had been more obliging.

But where was Raoul? He must be there somewhere, he could not afford to absent himself altogether, but though Halcyon peered to right and left through her screen of plants she could not see him.

The waltz came to an end and the dancers moved towards the chairs except for a few who remained on the floor waiting for the next number. No one invaded Halcyon's privacy until a stout gentleman in civilian garb, trousers and a long-tailed double-breasted jacket was lured by its coolness to seek refuge in the arcade.

He did not perceive Halcyon until he had sat down on the end of the long bench which she was occupying, then he struggled on to his feet again, and bowed:

'I apologise, mademoiselle, I did not perceive you—I had no wish to intrude.'

'You are not intruding. Please sit down, monsieur,' she said in her best French.

He subsided beside her. 'You are English, mademoiselle?' he asked in her own tongue.

She laughed. 'I'm afraid my accent betrayed me. I must admit I still don't speak your language very well. You're much better at mine.'

'It is necessary in my business.' He took off his mask and wiped his face with a large handkerchief. 'I grow too old for these capers,' he mourned. 'My wife will scold me.'

'Your wife is present?'

'She is somewhere around.' A gleam came into his faded blue eyes. 'I have escaped her vigilance with a gay young thing from Orléans, but *hélas*, she was too energetic for me. Odette will say it serves me right.' He sighed and replaced his handkerchief. 'We have come to pay our respects to *la petite* upon her name day. We knew the family well in Paris, but this dressing up!' He spread his hands. 'It may be very romantic, but it does not make for comfort.'

'Yours isn't very different from ordinary evening dress.'

'Which I never wear,' he confessed. 'I fear *mes amis les* Dubois go too high in the world for the Latours— that is my name, mademoiselle, Georges Latour—to ascend with them.'

'But France is a republic,' Halcyon reminded him mischievously. 'What of the famous French *égalité*?'

'A myth, mademoiselle, always there will be those who go up and those who come down, and there are still members of the *ancien régime* around. Do you see the lady who sits with our hostess? She could never be a *paysanne*. I hear Solange Dubois plans to marry *la petite* Mariette to her son.'

'I believe an engagement is imminent,' Halcyon said stoically, but why was not Raoul dancing with Mariette?

Georges Latour sighed. 'I think she makes the mistake. Mariette will not be happy out of her class. The noble lady will look down upon her.'

'I fancy Mariette can take care of herself,' Halcyon told him drily, 'and don't forget, she will hold the purse strings.'

'That is true.' Her companion became suddenly aware of her as a person. He turned in his seat to stare at her. The light filtering through the azaleas dappled her white dress and flickered on her bare arms and neck. He could not see her eyes for her mask, but now his had become accustomed to the dim light, he could discern her beautiful mouth and rounded chin, and the entrancing line of her throat and shoulder. The music had started again and couples were gyrating past them. He asked:

'Are you not dancing, mademoiselle?'

She shook her head. 'No, Monsieur Latour, I'm merely an onlooker. Later I shall slip away. It's very kind of you to talk to me.'

He seemed puzzled. 'It is not *comme il faut*,' he murmured. 'A beautiful *demoiselle* like yourself.' He half rose. 'If you would do me the honour?'

'Thank you, but no. I'm quite happy sitting here watching.'

'But have you no friends?'

'I'm staying in the chateau, and I helped with this pageant, so I wanted to see it, but the people here tonight are strangers to me.'

'The Dubois should have introduced you to some partners,' he said indignantly. 'Let me take you to my wife, she will find . . .'

'Thank you, but no again,' she interrupted. 'You are very kind, but I . . . I don't care for dancing.'

'But you should.' Her isolation was troubling the good-natured elderly man. Actually Halcyon loved dancing, but she had no wish to expose herself to the curious eyes of the Dubois' acquaintances. The one person she had expected to see did not appear to be present. She had wanted to behold Raoul in all his glory, even though the sight of him paying court to Mariette would have been a little painful. But another man was wearing the gorgeous costume designed for him, and she wondered a little anxiously if he were ill or had had an accident. She would have to dislodge her father and make him enquire for her, for she dared not do so herself.

Meanwhile, finding her unresponsive, her companion settled himself more comfortably in his seat and said:

'*Eh bien*, mademoiselle, it is as you wish. Myself, I could find nothing pleasanter than to sit here in the cool with such a charming companion.'

''Alcyone, at last! So this is where you have been hiding!'

Halcyon started violently. Preoccupied with her new anxiety and her companion's talk, she had ceased to watch the dancers, so had not noticed Raoul's approach, but as he could not have come through the barricade, he must have been searching the arcades. One lightning glance showed her that he had chosen a dress which made Murat's magnificent uniform look garish. Fawn trousers, black cutaway coat and frilled shirt were quiet and elegant. His hair was combed with a Byronic quiff, and through the narrow black mask his eyes gleamed dangerously.

'This is a masked ball,' she said calmly, though her heart had begun to race. 'You're not supposed to recognise anyone.'

'Such childish nonsense,' he exclaimed contemptuously. 'As if you could disguise yourself from me behind a scrap of black velvet!'

Georges Latour was beaming on them both delightedly.

'Aha, mademoiselle, you deceive the poor old man. You wait here for the coming of your *bien-aimé* and that is why you will not dance.'

'I didn't know he was here,' Halcyon stammered,

covered with confusion. Raoul was not her *bien-aimé*.

'*Eh bien*, you do now,' Raoul told her. '*Naturellement* I am here.'

'And you will dance with her?' Georges Latour asked eagerly.

'That is my intention.'

'*Bon*, and I will take myself to the bar,' Georges Latour said, heaving up his bulk.

'Don't hurry away,' Halcyon besought him. She could not allow Raoul to make her conspicuous, and Mariette would be furious. 'I said I didn't care for dancing.'

She glanced challengingly up at Raoul.

'I will leave Monsieur to persuade you otherwise,' Georges Latour returned with a grin, and lumbered away to find the bar.

Raoul did not waste time on persuasion, he simply took hold of Halcyon's wrists and pulled her to her feet.

'Come,' he said imperiously.

'But, Raoul...'

'Do I have to carry you on to the floor?'

'Don't be absurd, but really...'

Unheeding her protests, his arm encircled her waist and he marched her down the arcade and out on to the floor.

They moved well together, and throwing aside her scruples, Halcyon gave herself up to the sheer pleasure of waltzing on that excellent floor. After all, she was doing nothing very heinous. It was perfectly in order for Raoul to give her one dance since she knew nobody else there, even Mariette could not object to that ... or would she? Halcyon decided that it did not matter if she did, she would not spoil these perfect moments considering Mariette's reactions.

They passed the ladies on the dais and Madame de Valprès leaned forward to gaze at her son. Raoul flashed a brilliant smile up at her and she smiled back. Halcyon wondered if she knew who his partner was, but she did not seem perturbed that Raoul was not dancing with Mariette. Then she ceased to think about Madame de Valprès, Mariette or anybody else, but surrendered to the ecstasy of being in Raoul's arms and moving with him in complete accord over the smooth floor. He did not speak and she was glad he did not do so; commonplaces would break the magic that enfolded her. For a few blissful moments doubts and fears could be left in abeyance while she yielded to the intense attraction this man had for her.

The dance came to an end, and as the couples became disengaged, she gave a long sigh.

'That was perfect, Raoul. Thank you so much.'

He kept hold of her hand.

'Where are you going? Back to your elderly admirer?'

'No. He's busy sampling Monsieur Dubois' cognac. I shall return to my turret chamber. We are lodged in the South Tower. Perhaps you know it?'

'I do, but why must you run away? It's still early.'

She smiled sweetly. 'I've no reason to stay. After that dance, Monsieur Latour would be an anti-climax, and you've other obligations.'

'I fulfilled those before I found you.'

Yet she had not seen him on the floor, but then she had not expected to behold him in such sombre garb and might have missed him.

'All of them, monsieur?' she asked meaningly.

'All of them,' he declared firmly.

Mariette would be wondering where he was, or had they quarrelled? Possibly they had over the ridiculous

Murat uniform, but she was not going to provide the antidote to Mariette's ill humour. Withdrawing her hand from his, she dropped him a curtsey, said:

'*Bonne nuit*, Raoul,' and flitted away.

She threaded her way between the couples assembling for the next dance, and gained the doorway into the tower. No use looking back, the potted plants obscured the view of the ballroom. She closed the door behind her and began her ascent of the twisting stair.

About half way up, she realised she was being followed. The corkscrew steps were difficult enough to negotiate in her long dress without turning in her tracks to confront her pursuer, and she suspected who it was. He must be crazy to follow her, and when she reached the top and had got her breath, she would tell him so. Her thin slippers made little sound on the stones, but though he moved lightly his footsteps woke a hollow echo. To Halcyon they were the footsteps of fate. He could only be indulging in a sudden whim, a desire to renew his acquaintance with the geography of the castle, so she decided feverishly, but there was something ominous about those following footfalls.

The stair ended at a door which opened on to a square landing to which the three doors of their apartments had access, and the other broader staircase which joined the main one into the hall on the floor below. Halcyon stepped through it and turned to face her pursuer, breathing quickly, for her heart was beating fast, not only with the exertion of the climb but the anticipation of seeing Raoul.

He came through on to the landing, smiling wryly.

'Why such haste, *ma mie*, it was like chasing a chamois!'

'Why have you come?' she demanded.

The yellow eyes narrowed between his dark lashes.

'Since you are in occupation, it is an opportunity to see the view from the tower,' he said lightly. 'Usually my visits are confined to the state rooms, and I much prefer ... the towers.'

'Oh, well, if that's all.' She opened the door to the studio, wondering why she had felt so apprehensive. 'Come in and look at it.'

She switched on the light, which disclosed the bare room, looking more functional than inviting. Mariette's portrait was on the easel, a cloth covering it, her typewriter was on a bare wooden table. There were no easy chairs, only hard wooden ones, though that was not unusual. The French are not famed for comfortable seating. It is the custom for French families to sit round a table in the evenings on hard-backed chairs. Only in her salon had Madame Dubois introduced sofas and armchairs at her daughter's insistence.

'What a cheerless place,' Raoul said, looking round. He moved across to the narrow window. 'The view is the only thing to be said for it, and that tonight is overcast.' He turned back to Halcyon. 'Is this where you spend your time? Upon all the occasions when I have visited the chateau since you came here I've had no glimpse of you.'

'We don't live with the family,' she explained, 'and you came to see Mademoiselle Dubois, didn't you?'

'I came because I must,' he told her succinctly. He lifted the cloth from Félix's picture and Mariette's face smiled out at them.

'*Très bon*,' Raoul declared. 'He has caught her silly simper admirably.' He let the cloth fall. 'I am only surprised she did not insist upon wearing her tiara. Such ostentation!' His lip curled with distaste.

Halcyon moved uncomfortably. 'I don't think you should speak so scathingly about your ... hostess,' she rebuked him.

Raoul smiled cynically. 'We have no illusions about each other,' he returned. 'Has your father ever painted you?'

'Not a conventional portrait. He doesn't care for such work, his style is impressionistic. That,' she indicated the easel, 'is a bread-and-butter commission.'

'Then I hope Pierre Dubois makes it worth his while.'

'He will do. Won't you sit down?'

She seated herself behind her typewriter, while Raoul turned a chair about and sat down astride it, folding his arms along the back of it.

'But you, what do you do,' he asked, 'while Papa paints? Watch the world go by from your tower window like a Tennysonian heroine?'

'I'm surprised you know our English poets.'

'I was partly educated in England. Do you see only shadows, like the Lady of Shalott?'

'I'm much too busy to be so fanciful. I have my own work.'

He raised his eyebrows.

'You mean you manipulate that machine?'

'Except when Daddy finds the noise too irritating and then I have to carry on in longhand.'

'What is it you write? Poetry?'

She stared at him in surprise.

'Whatever made you suggest that? I'm sure I don't look in the least like a poetess, and there's no money in it.'

'So you write for money—you disappoint me. You have an elfin quality, my sylph, and I could imagine you composing exquisite verse.'

'How intriguing, but I'm much too substantial to be elfin.'

Raoul studied her through half-closed eyes, a gleam of tawny light between the shadows of his lashes. Halcyon began to sift through a sheaf of typewritten sheets, more to give occupation for her fingers and eyes than for any purpose. Far above the hall as they were, no sound reached them from the revelry below. Raoul looked devastatingly handsome, his costume emphasising his breadth of shoulder and narrow flanks; he also looked a little wicked. Halcyon was very conscious of their isolation and his intent regard disconcerted her.

'In that filmy gown of yours you look anything but substantial,' he told her dreamily. 'Water nymph, mountain sylph, or perhaps the wraith of one of those long-dead women who once inhabited this castle. You are a little like the unfortunate Antoinette. I have a miniature of her that was saved from the holocaust. She was only a de Valprès by marriage, so she did not bear the family features.' He stroked his own impressive nose. 'She had your look of wide-eyed innocence for all she was a mother. I wonder if you have ever seen her ghost? She could have watched the approach of the *sans-culottes* through that very window coming to haul her off to doom, poor, pretty creature.'

Halcyon shivered slightly at this suggestion.

'Is she supposed to haunt this tower?' she asked uneasily.

'No, nor anywhere else. If she haunted any spot it should be the Roman bath, though in her day it was not fit for use, nor were the willows planted, but even then I believe it was a favourite place for ... assignations.'

The wicked glint in his eyes became more pronounced and Halcyon was sure he was recalling his first meeting with herself, but that had not been an assignation, only a chance encounter.

'I hoped I might find you there again,' he said softly.

'It's out of bounds now the Dubois are in residence.'

'*Malheureusement!* And of course you obey their edicts.'

'Of course.'

'Someone more enterprising might not.' She made no reply to this implication and he shifted his position on the hard chair. 'What made you, for I understand you had a major part in the proceedings, choose the Empire period? The earlier age was more picturesque with its white wigs and brocade coats. You could have impersonated Antoinette very effectively.'

'Mademoiselle Dubois would have wanted to do that.' He made a grimace. 'But I didn't choose the period, it was Monsieur Dubois' idea, and the Empire dresses for the women at least were easier than hooped skirts—besides, I know much more about the Napoleonic era, I'm writing about it now.'

She touched her sheets of manuscript.

'You are what?'

'Writing a novel. My line is light romance, historical romance. I've had a small success with my first two. This is my third.'

His eyes widened in astonishment.

'*Mon Dieu,* so my sylph is a *femme savante!*'

'Hardly that. I don't depict the period in any depth. All that is required is a superficial background, a love story and plenty of light repartee.'

'I can believe you are good at that. You have a sharp tongue, 'Alcyone, but as for the love story, are you then an expert in the tender passion?'

He was mocking her now, his golden eyes glinting with derision.

'That again doesn't need to be explored too profoundly.' She folded her hands on the typewriter cover, and declared demurely: 'You see, my heroines have to be pure.'

'Which must limit your scope.'

'All to the good. As you've implied, my experience is limited.'

He leaned forward over his folded arms, his voice insinuating.

'It could be ... enlarged.'

'There's no necessity.' She stood up. 'I can't offer you a drink, but I can make you some coffee.'

Raoul sprang to his feet.

'*Ciel*, I am forgetting. You have had no supper.'

'It doesn't matter, I'm not hungry.' Halcyon had a fleeting vision of the appetising spread in the buffet next to the ballroom, which she had seen being prepared earlier in the day, and having a healthy girl's appetite, smiled a little ruefully. But even if Raoul were to suggest it, no dishes however delicious would tempt her to return to the mob below.

'But don't let me keep you from yours,' she went on politely. 'I understand Monsieur Dubois' chef has excelled himself over the cold collations.'

'Has he indeed? I will go and investigate.' Raoul moved towards the door. 'You are staying here?'

'Yes. *Bonne nuit*, Raoul, and good eating.'

Her smile was a little forlorn, the room would seem dreary when he had gone.

'*Au 'voir, chérie*,' he said carelessly, and bowed in a manner suited to his dress.

As the door closed behind him, Halcyon sat down again and idly turned the typed sheets in front of her. She felt deserted, yet she could hardly have expected Raoul to remain, but his departure had been almost precipitate. The lure of supper had been too strong to incline him to stay longer, and of course he would have to be present when the announcement of his engagement was made. At least she had escaped that.

Her eyes fell upon the sheet she was holding ... 'a thatch of thick black hair above strange tawny eyes, almost golden' ... it was the description of her hero, who had metamorphosed from blond to dark. She picked up a pencil and scored it through, substituting brown hair and grey eyes. Though it might enhance her interpretation of her hero's feelings, or more correctly what her heroine interpreted them to be, she could not afford to cast him in Raoul's mould. The whole thing would become too personal, though already he had added colour to her love scenes. She leaned her head pensively upon her cupped hand. It was easy but painful to imagine herself-cum-heroine in Raoul's embrace, but such a situation might well endanger the lady's precious chastity. She was not so stupid that she did not realise that she had some sort of attraction for him, but with the negotiations for marriage to Mariette already in hand he could not offer her a legal union, and such she was sure was far from his thoughts. Being an amorous Frenchman he was possibly considering an affair, but that almost under Mariette's nose was not complimentary to either of them, and she would not consent to it under any circumstances. She checked her racing thoughts. Because Raoul had paid her a little attention, had danced with her, it was absurd to imagine he had any thought of going any further.

A tap on the door startled her out of her reverie.

'Come in,' she called mechanically.

To her astonishment Raoul came back into the room, carrying a bottle, which he placed carefully on the table beside her.

'I think you will find this more suitable to a festive

evening than coffee,' he told her, smiling. She saw it was champagne.

Another tap on the door, and at his imperious '*Entrez*' one of the hired waiters appeared carrying a large tray. Raoul lifted the typewriter and deposited it on the floor, so the man could put his burden on the table. He handed him a roll of notes and the man bowed himself out obsequiously with a conspiratorial grin, as Raoul swept the covering cloth off the tray.

'Our supper, madame, and I hope you are not too much of a wraith to do justice to it.'

'Oh, Raoul, and I thought you'd gone!'

'You misjudged me.' His face became suddenly grave. 'Be careful you do not do so in more important matters.'

Halcyon looked up from surveying the spread—scallop shells filled with a concoction of lobster; shrimp, mushroom and chicken patties, petits fours, glasses containing a mouthwatering mixture of fruit, ice and cream.

'I'll endeavour not to do so,' she said. 'Though I don't altogether understand you.'

'How should you? I am an *homme du monde*, and you, *chérie*, a mere novice on the threshold of life, but at least always give me the benefit of the doubt.' He was busy opening the bottle of champagne. 'You have wine glasses?'

'Yes, some very ordinary ones.' She went to fetch them from a corner cupboard, considering what he had said, but as she returned with them, he laughed at her solemn expression.

'No more profundity,' he decreed. 'We will be gay.'

He filled a glass and handed it to her.

'We will play a little game, we are the Comte and Comtesse des Saules before the revolution and the chateau is all ours. *Madame ma femme*, I salute you.'

She drank, though she found his choice of make-believe a little painful. She would never be his wife and the chateau could only be his through Mariette. But he seemed unaware of any incongruity in his fantasy, which he continued to act with verve. She became infected with his gaiety and sparkled, matching him in bright repartee. They were as carefree as two children enjoying a secret midnight feast.

'Will Monsieur le Comte partake of this excellent confection of fruit and ice?' she asked demurely, having eaten her fill of savouries.

'*Non*, madame. Eat it yourself, sweets to the sweet, but I provide the spice.' His eyes were eloquent.

The champagne went a little to Halcyon's head. Over her second, or was it her third? glass of champagne, she told him:

'We should drink to Mariette's health and happiness, for after all, this evening is being held in her honour.'

'Certainly,' he agreed, lifting his glass. 'Here's to her long life, prosperity and a loving husband.'

He drained the wineglass, set it down and looked at her audaciously.

'Shall I drink the same toast to you, *chérie*?'

'I think you've drunk enough champagne, and so have I.'

'How censorious you sound!' He tilted the bottle. 'There is not a lot left, we might as well finish it.'

'No more for me.' She put her hand over her glass. 'I don't want to become tipsy.'

'There is only myself to witness your tipsiness. What form does it take? Do you become loquacious, maudlin or merely giggly?'

'I don't know. I've never been in that state.'

'There is always a first time. It might do you good to break through your inhibitions.'

She darted a suspicious glance at him. Had he an object in view by urging her to drink? His face expressed only bland curiosity, but the tawny eyes held a mischievous gleam.

'Sorry to disappoint you, but in the present situation I prefer to keep my head,' she told him.

'You always do, *n'est-ce pas*? The cool, collected English Miss. I realise the obvious tactics are useless with you. I shall have to be more subtle.'

She leaned towards him, her eyes big and serious.

'What do you want of me, Monsieur de Valprès?'

'Everything,' he said promptly. 'All that a woman can give a man.' Spoken lightly, almost casually, but there was a flicker of flame in his regard.

Halcyon drew back, regretting her question.

'That's a tall order!'

'I know it is, but I am a patient man. I can wait. I usually get what I want.'

'Isn't your greatest desire to own the Chateau des Saules?' she asked deliberately.

A change came over him. The bantering laughter died out of his face and eyes. He looked round the stone walls of the tower with a brooding gaze.

'The price may prove too high,' he murmured. 'I am not sure I can pay it.'

'Of course you can.' Halcyon lashed herself with the pain of her own probing. She must remind him that he was not free if he intended to pursue the course to which he was committed, already he was endangering his position with Mariette by dallying with her. 'All that is required of you is your signature to a marriage contract, which, being French, you'll break at your convenience.'

Raoul smiled lazily. 'Frenchmen do not hold a monopoly in infidelity,' he observed. 'Italians are worse.' His lips twitched. 'Would you be willing to assist me to break it?'

'Certainly not,' she declared firmly.

'*Eh bien*, this is an unsuitable theme for an evening's entertainment,' he remarked with a return to his flippant manner.

'It happens to be pertinent, but it must be very late. Have you the time?'

There was no clock in the studio. Raoul glanced of habit at his wrist and shrugged his shoulders. 'Alas, no. Wristwatches are not of the Empire period, you see.'

She had not worn hers for the same reason. She stood up uncertainly; there was a travel clock by her bed, but she was unwilling to go into her bedroom in case he followed her, though she might be misjudging him, as he had asked her not to do.

At that moment the studio door was flung open and Felix stumbled in accompanied by the waiter who had brought up their feast. The man had come to collect the tray.

'*Merci, merci*,' Felix mumbled. 'So lucky you were there to help me upstairs.' He collapsed into a chair. 'My dear, I've been celebrating a little too copiously, but it isn't often so much good cheer can be had for free.'

'That's just as well,' Halcyon said sharply.

The waiter collected his tray and he gave Raoul a sympathetic glance as he went out. It was too bad the generous Monsieur was to be baulked by the father's inopportune appearance.

Felix became aware of Raoul's presence.

'Good lord!' he exclaimed. 'What on earth are you doing here? Your mother left hours ago, and the Du-

98

bois gave out you'd gone with her because she wasn't well, to save their faces. Had a tiff with the girl-friend?'

He looked at the champagne bottle and glasses, from whence his glance went to his daughter's conscious face and Raoul's expressionless one. 'Will someone tell me what's going on?' he demanded peevishly.

'Nothing is going on,' Raoul said coolly. 'Your daughter had had enough of the ball, so I had a little supper sent up to her. But it must be very late, so I will say good night.' He smiled at Halcyon. 'I am glad you revealed to me the staircase in the turret, so I can slip out unobserved since I am not supposed to be here.'

He bowed to them both and was gone.

Felix stared at Halcyon owlishly.

'Do you know it's after midnight? Has he been here all the time with you?'

'Most of it,' she admitted unwillingly.

Felix roared with laughter, slapping his thigh.

'Well, you're a deep one! Mariette has been waiting all night for him to apologise and come to claim her. She'll be hopping mad when she hears where he was.'

'I hope she never does,' Halcyon said quickly.

'Well, perhaps not if that waiter chap holds his tongue, and I expect de Valprès has paid him to do so.' He suddenly sobered. 'Hal, you're not ... you haven't...?'

'No, Daddy,' she told him quietly. 'It was as Raoul said, I came up here and he brought me some supper.'

'Very obliging of him.' He sighed. 'We seem to get deeper into his debt every day, but I advise you to watch your step, my girl. I don't trust Frenchmen with women.'

'Oh, it's all right, Daddy, Raoul and I understand

each other.'

But did they? Had she made it clear she was not available? Raoul had said he wanted all she had to give and he was prepared to wait. She could only hope it was the champagne speaking through him, and tomorrow he would have forgotten what he had said.

CHAPTER SIX

A FEW days later the Greys returned to Le Nid. Monsieur Blum showed them round with pride and many a curious glance at Halcyon, but of Raoul there was no sign. Since Mariette parted with them on friendly terms it would seem she had no inkling of where her errant suitor had spent the major part of the evening of the dance. As Felix had said, it was generally assumed that Madame de Valprès had been unwell and he had taken her home.

If Pierre Dubois was disappointed that the expected *dénouement* to his lavish hospitality had not materialised, he gave no hint of it. Felix told Halcyon he had gathered that they had ascribed the hitch in their plans to a silly tiff between the couple over Raoul's refusal to wear the Murat dress and were expecting that the breach would be soon healed.

The weather turned very hot, the river shrinking to a sluggish stream between banks of sand in the drought. The vegetation wilted, only the weeping willows watered by the never-failing spring that fed the Roman bath retained their freshness. Halcyon glimpsed from afar the tops of the coloured umbrellas erected by the pool for the benefit of the Dubois family and their guests.

The Greys' connection with the chateau was terminated. Felix's pictures of the building and Mariette had been delivered and paid for, thus disposing of any financial worries for the rest of the year, the portraits in the gallery had been renovated, so they had no occasion to go there.

Halcyon spent the first week of her return in a state of feverish expectancy, anticipating that Raoul might call. She knew now that she had fallen hopelessly in love with him and both longed for and dreaded his reappearance, but he did not come and she concluded that he regretted his indiscreet behaviour at the dance, and had decided to avoid her in future. He was not the sort of man to allow a passing fancy for a penniless girl to jeopardise his carefully laid plans.

But if Raoul did not come, another did, for with their return to the cottage, Louis resumed his visits, sometimes taking Felix off for the day to paint some scene that had caught his interest, but more often he hung about the cottage, cadging meals, hindering Halcyon and irritating her with his sentimental glances. She made herself very busy, cleaning, cooking and even tackling the neglected patch of garden behind the house, though her novel still hung fire. Resolutely she tried by these occupations to keep her thoughts from straying towards Raoul de Valprès. That was over, finished, an evening of glamour to look back upon in the days to come, but for the present, while she was still in his vicinity, it was better not to dwell either upon that night or their former meetings.

In spite of all her efforts she could not wholly banish him; some object, a chance word would recall him to mind, and at night, before she slept, his face would swim before her closed eyes, the haughty profile, the languorous glance of his tawny eyes between his thick lashes, when he looked at her, the soft inflection of his voice when he had called her 'chérie'. Oh, Raoul de Valprès knew only too well how to win a woman's heart, and now he would be applying the same technique to win Mariette—and her chateau. But still the engagement had not been announced.

Though Halcyon had no pretext to visit the chateau, Felix sometimes went there. He was painting the historic willows, but in his own style, which meant they were hardly recognisable as willow trees. Mariette often came to speak to him and from her he learned, and passed the informationon to his daughter, that the young man who had obliged by wearing the Murat uniform was still staying there, and his attentions to the daughter of the house had brought Raoul to heel. Felix had occasionally glimpsed the three of them disporting themselves in the Roman bath, though as he remarked, Mariette was more often reclining in a bikini on a lilo set beneath the umbrellas than in the water.

'She's coaxing me to paint her like that, but so far I haven't risen,' Felix told her. 'I'd rather paint de Valprès, he has a beautiful body without his clothes. I'm sure he's realised that if he doesn't pander to Mariette's whims he'll lose her.'

'Then why doesn't he clinch the deal and become engaged?' Halcyon asked, stifling the pang her father's words had given her. 'Or is it Mademoiselle Dubois who is stalling?'

'I shouldn't think so, he's crazy about him, but de Valprès——' Felix shrugged his shoulders. 'I can't fathom that fellow at all.'

In the light of Raoul's unflattering remarks when he saw Mariette's portrait, Halcyon thought perhaps she could. Raoul wanted the Chateau des Saules, but he was reluctant to accept the bride that went with it. She told herself that she despised him for his mercenary motives, and pitied Mariette, but she knew in her secret heart that she envied her, and in her place would have accepted Raoul on any terms if his proposal was honourable. She was not sure that she could hold out against an illicit one, so it was as well that he had lost interest in herself.

One sunny morning, Felix betook himself to the willow trees with a packed lunch, intending to spend the day there. As it was a little cooler with a fresh breeze blowing, Halcyon decided to have a big bake during his absence, for the new electric cooker was still a delightful novelty. She would make a fruit pie for dinner that night, tartlets for a standby, scones, a sponge and a fruit cake. She was rolling out pastry when, somewhat to her annoyance, Louis came strolling in through the open back door. For once he was wearing a clean shirt and his hair and beard were trimmed and combed. He had come, she anticipated, in the hope that she would be preparing coffee for elevenses. She tried not to feel peeved by his appearance, for the man had few friends and was, she suspected, lonely. Mercifully she need not stand on ceremony with him.

'Please excuse me, but I must get on,' she told him, after a perfunctory greeting, 'the oven's just right. When I've done, I'll make you some coffee.'

'That's all right, Hal, I like watching you work.'

She wore a flowered overall, and a mob cap to protect her hair from flour. Her sleeves were rolled up past her elbows, showing her arms delicately tinted by the sun to a pale apricot, her long dark lashes made little shadows on her peach-bloom cheeks, slightly flushed by her exertions as she looked down at her task. With the removal of her hair under the cap, the fine lines of her jaw and throat were in evidence; she looked slim, young and endearingly intent, a charming domestic picture.

Louis lounged against the edge of the table observing her, while he remarked:

'I should be going down to Provence, pictures of the Bridge at Avignon and the Pont du Gard always sell well, and the weather is just right for camping out.'

'Then why don't you go?'

'Because I can't tear myself away from you.'

Halcyon sighed. She put her first batch in the oven before she attempted any rejoinder, while she decided that she would have to speak plainly.

'I'm afraid I've nothing to give you, Louis,' she said gently. 'And you mustn't neglect your work because of me. Perhaps it would be a good thing if you did go away and try to forget me.'

'I could never do that,' he declared vehemently. 'Hal, for you I'm ready to give up my way of life. My father would find me a position if I ... er ... conformed. I loathe conventional existence, but for you I'm prepared to endure it. I'm not a fool, I've been properly educated, and I could make good if I gave my mind to it.' He straightened himself and looked at her eagerly. 'What do you say, Hal?'

'That it wouldn't work. I couldn't condemn you to a life you hated and in time you'd either give it up and run away, or you'd resent me for landing you in a rut and come to hate me too.'

'You're wrong, you must be wrong,' he said insistently. 'Any sacrifice I made would be amply compensated for if you would marry me.'

'I'm not worth sacrifices, Louis.'

'Oh, but you are. I've watched you day by day, the way you look after your father, the efficiency with which you run the house, and you're a good girl, Hal. I may tell you I've met many who aren't. This permissiveness ...' He shrugged his shoulders. 'I wouldn't be a man if I didn't occasionally take advantage of what is offered to me. But I don't respect those girls, not like I do you, Hal. You haven't had an easy time, I can see that, and if I get this position my father is always offering, I could give you comfort and security.'

He looked at her pleadingly, and Halcyon was touched, but he was, she thought, being optimistic. He had lived a wandering life too long to be able to settle down to respectability, but she had not the heart to point that out.

'I'd even shave off my beard and cut my hair to please you,' Louis added.

'Thank you, Louis,' Halcyon said sincerely. 'I ... I'm honoured,' she smiled faintly. 'That's the right word, isn't it? That you're prepared to do so much for me. But it's no use, because I don't love you, and I'd only marry a man I did.'

She glanced at her watch and turned hastily to the oven to draw out the scones and the sponge. The latter was a rich golden brown, the scones risen to perfection. Next she would put in the pastry, and finally the cake.

'I wish you'd give me your whole attention,' Louis complained peevishly.

Guiltily aware that her mind was more on her cooking than on him, she said:

'Sorry, but I told you I must get my baking done. Have a scone?'

'No, thank you,' he almost shouted. 'I know what's turned you against me! It's while you've been at that damned chateau. You met someone at the ball, didn't you? Someone who's given you elevated ideas, so I'm not good enough for you now. But he'll let you down, Hal, that sort always do.'

He was near enough to the truth to cause Halcyon to change colour. She hastened to put her pastry in the oven, hoping the heat from it would account for her flushed cheeks. As she turned about she found him confronting her with a feverish glitter in his eyes.

'I won't take no for an answer, Hal. Marry me and you'll learn to love me. I'll make you love me.'

'Please, Louis ...' She sought to fend him off, but now thoroughly aroused, he caught her in his arms, bearing her back against the table.

'I've waited and waited,' he said through his teeth, 'and I've heard all the rumours about de Valprès.' Halcyon started. 'His horse tied to your paling—why he has so concerned himself with Le Nid. I didn't believe them, but now it seems they're true. If you can give that Casanova your favours you can't be all that particular, and I'll have my share!'

His hot breath was on her face, and she was helpless in his hold. Her cap fell off and her hair fell in a wild tangle on to her shoulders, as she struggled to evade his lips, but before his mouth touched hers, a cool, ironical voice from the open door drove them apart.

'What a charming picture! I am afraid I have arrived at an inopportune moment.'

Louis spun round to face the intruder, while Halcyon was overwhelmed by intense dismay. Her hands flew to her disordered hair, pushing it away from her face. Against her better judgment, she had longed for Raoul to call upon them, had in fact persuaded herself that he never would, and now he was here, having arrived at a most unfortunate moment. She could have slain Louis cheerfully for placing her in an ignominious and embarrassing situation.

'It isn't ... what you're thinking,' she said lamely.

Louis had noted her confusion and believed he saw a chance to score off de Valprès, whom he considered to be his rival. He laughed derisively.

'What else could it be, *chérie*?' he asked maliciously. He turned to Raoul. 'You should knock, monsieur, to proclaim your presence.'

'The door was wide open,' Raoul pointed out.

'So it was. Hal and I are very old friends and we have an understanding, soon I hope to ripen into a closer relationship. But I should have closed the door.'

'You should,' Raoul agreed blandly, but his eyes were glittering balefully in the brown mask of his face. 'I always make sure the doors are shut, and preferably locked, before I kiss a girl.'

He was wearing his riding clothes, he must have ridden to Gracedieu, and now Halcyon could hear Saracen's familiar sounds of impatience. The hand that held Raoul's riding crop was white with the force of his restraint. Halcyon suspected that he would have liked to use it upon Louis ... or upon herself.

'Kisses between us are so commonplace,' Louis observed airily, 'I would be shutting doors all the time.'

'Louis, don't lie!' Halcyon cried angrily. 'You know I won't allow...'

'But you do, *chérie*,' he said softly. 'De Valprès must know that I practically live here, and that by your invitation. Oh, of course, when Papa is around we're more circumspect, but I met him en route for the chateau where he is spending the day.'

So Louis had known she would be alone, and had deliberately taken advantage of the fact. She turned in desperate appeal to the other man.

'Louis is trying to give you a wrong impression...'

'Or are you?' Raoul interrupted coldly. 'Appearances support his assertions.' He looked at the table. During her struggle with Louis, the scones had been scattered, the sponge flattened. 'I am afraid your culinary efforts have been spoiled by your ardour.'

'Oh, go away, both of you!' Halcyon cried vehemently, feeling the destruction of her cooking was the last straw. 'Leave me alone!'

'I'm going,' Louis announced jauntily. 'See you this evening, *mignonne*, where we can carry on where we left off before this gentleman interrupted us. *Adieu*, Monsieur de Valprès.'

He sauntered out jauntily, whistling gaily, triumphant that he had managed to score off such an impressive rival.

Halcyon dropped on to one of the hard chairs and covered her face with her hands. She had not taken in the implication of Louis' last words, she had been too concerned with the havoc he had wrought. Tears of vexation forced themselves between her fingers, as she wailed:

'My beautiful cooking all ruined!'

'That is not all that is ruined,' Raoul said.

She had believed that he had also gone, and at the strange note in his voice, she raised her tear-stained face, startled to find him still there.

'What do you mean?' she asked.

He shrugged his shoulders. 'Only that a delightful idyll has been shattered, but it is of no more importance than your cakes.'

She stared at him uncomprehendingly, her eyes green wells in her pale face.

'Raoul, you can't really believe there's anything serious between Louis and me?'

His lip curled fastidiously.

'Louis? Is that his name? As he said, I have been told he is always here and now I know why. I do not think much of your taste, Mademoiselle Grey, and I notice you have been careful never to mention him to me. An artist, isn't he, with casual morals, or so I have

109

heard. No doubt you become bored in your father's absences.' There was a bitter edge to his voice that she was at a loss to understand. 'And he offers amorous amusement to while the time away, but I thought...' He broke off and switched aimlessly at the table with his crop.

'I've never indulged in that sort of amusement,' Halcyon cried scornfully.

'Your *beau* seemed to think otherwise.'

Stung by the injustice he was doing her, Halcyon said what would have been better unsaid.

'You've no right to criticise my conduct, what about your own?'

For he had not made overtures to her when practically engaged to another girl?

Raoul de Valprès bowed with exaggerated courtesy.

'I would not presume to criticise you, 'Alcyone, and my conduct is my own affair. I hoped for a very different reception, but it is as well I should see you as you really are.' He smiled wryly. 'Willow trees and romantic towers have a lot to answer for.'

'But, Raoul ...' She moved towards him, her eyes beseeching.

He waved her back with a long brown hand. 'It is useless to try your siren's wiles upon me, I have become impervious to them. *Adieu*, my ...' He bit his lip, turned upon his heel and went swiftly out of the open door.

'Raoul, stop!' Halcyon rushed after him, pride and dignity forgotten. She could not let him go believing Louis was her lover. Her overall pocket caught on the latch of the door, by the time she had torn it free, she was too late. All she saw was Saracen's rump as he rode away at a sharp trot and her despairing cry was lost in the clatter of the horse's hooves.

She returned to the kitchen to be greeted by a smell of burning, and drew from the oven the charred remnants of her pie and tarts. This final disaster provoked no more tears. Though grieved by the waste of so much good ingredients, she settled down doggedly to making a fresh batch, while she mentally reviewed what had just occurred. Although Louis' malicious misrepresentation had been painful to her, it did not quite account for Raoul's bitterness while upbraiding her, for after all, what was it to do with him? He was deeply involved with another girl, and his appearance today had merely been a casual call *en passant*. She could only surmise that his vanity had been touched when he discovered he was, apparently, superseded in her favour by another man. Raoul de Valprès believed himself to be all-conquering where women were concerned, and had expected her to sit moping until he condescended to throw her a kind word. That the situation had been something like that flicked her pride. She *had* been moping and yearning for a sight of him, but she would do so no longer. She could even be grateful to Louis for driving him away. No girl could gain anything except humiliation by fretting for another woman's man.

Felix completed his picture of the willow trees. Though far from conventional, it had something, Halcyon was forced to admit. He had caught the graceful droop of the falling fronds, which gave an odd impression of a woman's tresses, and the composition breathed a nostalgic air.

'They are a memorial to a dead girl,' Felix reminded her, adding inconsequently, 'They would have sheared her hair before they cut off her head.'

So the resemblance to a woman's locks was deliberate.

After that, Felix became restless, complaining that he had painted everything in the environment that appealed to him. Louis did not come to Le Nid again, but Halcyon knew he met her father at the bistro in the evenings. Felix began to talk about the beauties of Provence, the old buildings in Arles and Nîmes, the grandeur of the Pont du Gard. Halcyon knew where this was tending, and pointed out that they could hardly leave the cottage now that de Valprès had done so much to make it more comfortable for them.

'Rubbish,' Felix growled, 'with August coming up he can let it far more profitably to summer visitors. You know very well Blum considers what we pay is chickenfeed. I find the suggestion of charity offensive, if you don't, and I expect de Valprès is regretting his generosity now his fancy for you has evaporated.'

'Then do you propose I come with you to Provence?' Halcyon asked, wincing from his hurtful words.

Felix was evasive. He thought of camping, which would be too rough for her. Halcyon gathered that he was going with Louis.

'I'll come back for you when the weather is cooler,' he told her. 'We can get another lodging somewhere.'

Halcyon sighed. She knew she had been optimistic to expect her father to settle anywhere; neither poverty nor insecurity really troubled him, but he hated having to stay put.

'Well, I suppose I could get a room somewhere in a village while I'm waiting for you,' Halcyon said regretfully, looking sadly round the bright little kitchen, that had been so much improved by the installation of electricity. She had grown fond of Le Nid.

'Perhaps Dubois could put you up at the chateau?' Felix suggested cheerfully. 'With Mariette's wedding coming up she could probably use your services as a secretary. There'll be a lot of correspondence and what-not. I'll ask him.'

'Don't you dare!' Halcyon said fiercely. The one place she would not go to was the Chateau des Saules. She asked tentatively: 'The engagement has been announced?'

Felix shrugged his shoulders. 'It's a foregone conclusion now she's got over his neglect at the ball.' He chuckled. 'Lucky she never discovered he was with you.' Halcyon blushed, and her father looked at her shrewdly. 'Surely you're too sensible to hanker after that young rip? Oh, I'll admit he's a girl's dream, but such men are totally unreliable and when they do marry they wed where the money is.'

'Of course I know all that, and I'm not hankering after Raoul; all the same, I wouldn't want to lodge with the Dubois. We're incompatible.'

Would she ever be able to forget the night of the dance? Raoul in the tower, their gaiety and mutual enjoyment, his slim figure so well set off by his elegant clothes, his dark handsomeness. That night he had deserted Mariette for her, risked all his prospects for an illicit midnight feast. She wondered as she had done many times before what he had come to say when he had surprised her with Louis, for there had been no need for him to call. Was it only a polite enquiry or had he had some other reason? Since then he had given all his attention to Mariette and no doubt she had been saved a great deal of heartache.

'Go to Provence if you really want to,' she told her father. 'But I'll stop here. We've just paid a month's rent, after a week or two you may be glad to come back.'

'You can't stay in the cottage alone.' Felix seemed to be suffering from some paternal qualms, or possibly he distrusted her proximity to the de Valprès vineyards. They argued for some time and the matter was still unsettled when a quite unexpected development occurred.

One morning the de Valprès car stopped at the gate of Le Nid, and Madame herself alighted from it. Cécile de Valprès was vigorous for her years and could drive a car as well as her son could. As Felix was hard at work, or appeared to be so, Halcyon took her into the kitchen.

'My father uses the sitting room for a studio,' she explained, 'so we live in the kitchen.'

'It is charming,' Madame told her, 'so homely.'

Halcyon looked at her doubtfully; that word could cover so much. 'I am glad my son arranged for the electricity to be installed,' the visitor went on. 'It must be much more convenient.'

'It is,' Halcyon agreed fervently.

Madame de Valprès sat down on one of the hard wooden chairs. At the chateau on the night of the ball she had looked the epitome of elegance, but this morning she wore trousers, a smock and an old straw hat, and but for her aristocratic features and long, supple fingers, she might have been a peasant out of her own vineyards. Yet so regal was her bearing, no one could mistake her for other than she was.

'I have been talking to a certain Louis Perron,' she said; her English was almost accentless, but she did not use idioms. 'An able artist. I am always willing to encourage artists. I understand he wishes to accompany your father on a tour of Provence. Is that not so?'

'Yes, Daddy wants to paint the Pont du Gard.'

Cécile de Valprès laughed, clear silvery laughter, and Halcyon warmed towards her.

'As if it had not been painted far too often already,

together with the Pont d'Avignon. I hope he will find more original subjects. But if he goes with Monsieur Perron you will be left alone.'

'I'll be all right, madame,' Halcyon hastened to assure her. 'I must get a move on with my own work which I've been neglecting, and I'm not nervous or anything like that.'

'But it is not fitting that a *jeune fille* should be without protection.'

Halcyon shrugged indifferently. 'No one here would harm me.'

'But people might gossip. I can offer you a better arrangement, and that is why I have come. Raoul says' —Halcyon strove not to look conscious at the mention of his name—'you are proficient with a typewriter. I have much clerical work to do in connection with the estate, invoices and correspondence, and my secretary has been taken ill. She has to have a long vacation. If you could take her place, while she is away, you would greatly oblige me and have somewhere to stay while your father is absent.'

'It's very kind of you to think of me, madame.' Halcyon was taken aback by this unexpected proposition. 'But surely you can find someone more efficient than I should be.'

'Not in a rural place like this,' Cécile told her. 'And I do not wish to obtain someone from Paris. Town girls are always so discontented in the country, but you like it.'

'I do indeed, but this post, if I accept it, would I have to live in?'

'Certainly, it would be more *comme il faut*.'

Halcyon sighed. Madame de Valprès was of an older generation, she still respected the conventions and she knew it would be useless to argue with her. Though her heart had leapt when she had been invited to Raoul's home, she knew it was the last place where she should go. He had ignored her existence since he had found her with Louis, but it was possible what had been between them might start up again if they were in daily contact.

Cécile de Valprès was watching her closely with a quizzical expression so like her son's that Halcyon was vaguely embarrassed. As if she sensed what was in the girl's mind, she told her:

'My son does not live with me. He has his own chalet. He visits me in the evenings when I assume you will wish to do your own work. I am told that you are an author?'

'Only a very humble one.'

'All creative work is worthy of respect,' Madame observed sententiously. She moved uncomfortably on the hard chair. 'I shall not overburden you with labour. We keep horses and I know that you ride.' She gave Halcyon a slightly malicious smile, and the girl surmised that she had been told of the incident of her wounded foot. Raoul seemed to have briefed her very thoroughly about her. 'You shall have a mount at your disposal. The early morning is the best time for such exercise at this time of year, so you can ride before you start work. We have a patio with a swimming pool. You also swim?'

'Yes. You make it all sound delightful.' She was tempted, but she hesitated. She would still be too close to Raoul.

'The cottage can be closed until you are ready to return to it,' Madame went on. 'It is hardly worth while trying to sublet it.'

'I ... I'll think about it,' Halcyon said. 'I'll have to consult my father.'

'I am sure Monsieur Grey will be agreeable,' Madame de Valprès said smoothly. 'Cannot you decide now? If you do not wish to come, I must find somebody else at once. The correspondence accumulates so fast.'

A statement from which Halcyon deduced that Madame de Valprès really did need clerical assistance and the position was not an invention of Raoul's, as for one wild moment she had suspected. Her father's jibe about their indebtedness to him had rankled and she did not wish to be under any further obligation to him, but if her services would be a help to his mother, it would be an opportunity for her to make some sort of repayment.

'If you're sure you really need me . . .' she began hesitantly.

'*Naturellement* I need you,' Madame intervened briskly. 'Why else should I ask you?' An ironic twinkle came into her shrewd dark eyes. 'I study my own convenience, mademoiselle, and I am not a philanthropist as my son appears to be.'

She looked pointedly at the electric cooker.

Halcyon flushed. Her visitor was evidently well aware of what Raoul had had done for them and was possibly critical of his generosity. To serve her in this emergency would only be a slight return for the transformation of Le Nid, bluntly she said so.

'That is a very nice way for you to feel about it,' Cécile de Valprès told her graciously. 'Gratitude is so rare, most young people nowadays grab all they can get without a thought of reciprocation. But you I see have a sense of what we used to call *noblesse oblige*. I think we should get on well together.'

Halcyon had not meant to commit herself without further consideration, the connection with Raoul was still troubling her, but Madame de Valprès seemed to think she had. She raised one or two minor points which might be construed into objections, but Madame soon settled them.

'When does your father leave?' she asked finally. 'I should like you to come as soon as possible.'

Felix had not fixed a date, but Halcyon knew he would be off at once if arrangements could be made for her. She also knew that Madame de Valprès' offer would have his wholehearted approval.

Feeling the occasion justified an interruption, she went to call him, and found he was not working, but doodling discontentedly upon a piece of drawing paper. He came with alacrity when she had explained what was toward, and with a feeling of unreality, her departure and his were settled for the day after the morrow.

Bellevue, as the de Valprès' place was called, justified its name. Situated where the ground began to rise towards the hills in which the river had its source, the whole valley was spread below it, the towers of the Chateau des Saules looking dwarfed in the distance. The slopes upon which the vines grew were terraced, but round the houses was level ground, terminating in a wood. The de Valprès owned a considerable stretch of woodland.

The house itself was built Spanish fashion around the patio, in the centre of which was a small swimming pool. Her husband, Cécile told Halcyon, had been very fond of Spain and the house had been built to his specification. Only the central part where the entrance was had two floors, the long enclosing wings were single storeyed. Halcyon's two rooms, for her accommodation included a small sitting room, were in one of them with windows opening on to the patio. Most of the rooms except the *salle à manger* and the salon in the front of the house had blank walls on the outer side, which made for security.

A formal garden surrounded the house, the beds laid out between gravel paths with strictly disciplined bedding plants. In the patio cypresses in tubs were set along between the windows, but they too were severely pruned.

The stables were across the field beyond the garden, and were visible from the house, amid a stand of trees was the deep-eaved roof of Raoul's chalet, which Madame pointed out to Halcyon. If Bellevue was Spanish in design, his place appeared to be Swiss.

'When he marries he will come here and I shall move over there,' Cécile de Valprès told her. 'It is big enough for one person.'

Halcyon was about to say, 'But won't he be living at the Chateau?' and checked herself as it occurred to her that until Dubois *père* died the Chateau des Saules was his domicile, unless he was prepared to surrender it to his son-in-law beforehand. Naturally in the first rapture of early marriage Raoul would prefer to have his wife to himself in his own home. Rapture? Could there be any of that in a marriage of convenience?

As for her misgivings about meeting him again, an encounter seemed improbable, for Madame reiterated that he rarely came to the house before the evening when he liked to discuss the business of the day with her over dinner.

'You will not mind if I ask you to dine in your room?' Madame asked apologetically. 'It is the only time we have together.'

Halcyon assured her that she would not mind at all, suspecting that Cécile de Valprès was anxious to keep her apart from her son. She had probably heard rumours and though she had imported Halcyon for her own convenience she had no wish to bring about a situation which might endanger his engagement to Mariette Dubois. If only she knew, the girl thought sadly, Raoul despises me now and he will be no more anxious to meet me than I am to run into him.

Which was not wholly true, for Raoul still drew her like a magnet, and it was a little painful to be so near to him and yet be completely separated from him. Still more so to realise, as she came to do, that in all probability he had only consented to her engagement on the understanding that she should be kept out of his way.

CHAPTER SEVEN

HALCYON'S days followed a pleasant routine. As the weather had become almost unpleasantly hot, she took her ride as prescribed by Madame de Valprès very early in the morning, when the parched land was still dew-laden before it was exposed to the fierce rays of the sun that instantly licked it up. She returned to shower and change and then to join her employer for breakfast of coffee and croissants in the patio before starting the day's work.

After lunch, when it was hottest, they both took a siesta, a Spanish custom favoured by the defunct Monsieur de Valprès, in darkened rooms with the Venetian blinds drawn against the heat. This was followed by afternoon tea, and then a final check-up of the mail, which had to be put ready for the postman to collect in the morning. If she so desired, she could swim in the pool before her solitary dinner in her room, and during the rest of the evening she tried to concentrate upon her novel, but as she sat at her typewriter, with the glass doors open to the patio, her attention frequently wandered. She was listening for the sound of Raoul's voice, longing to catch a glimpse of him, for she knew he was actually in the house, but he never came out into the patio as she half hoped he might.

Her morning ride was supervised by the head groom, a brown, wiry gnome of a man called Jules who had been a jockey. He had once ridden a horse in the

English Grand National, as he never tired of telling her, and had a fair knowledge of English. He lived in a flat above the stable buildings, and possessed a wife and a small daughter of about five years old. The wife Halcyon saw occasionally, when she was spreading her family's bedding out to air on the balcony in front of her flat in the French fashion. She was much younger than her husband, but that again was usual in France. Even so, the little girl, Suzanne, had arrived almost when she had despaired of ever having a baby.

'She should have been a boy,' Jules told Halcyon disparagingly. 'A girl cannot be a jockey.'

In spite of her sex, Jules adored his daughter and was exceedingly proud of her looks, for Suzanne was a very pretty child with black hair curling round her oval face and merry dark eyes, above cheeks as round and red as an apple. Although not the boy Jules had wanted, she loved horses and was never happier than when her father placed her on the back of one of the animals in his care.

'She rode before she could walk,' he said fondly.

'By the time she's grown up women jockeys may be commonplace,' Halcyon told him consolingly. 'They've already begun.'

'But they'll never run in the big races,' Jules declared, shaking his head.

'I wouldn't put it past them,' Halcyon laughed.

Suzanne took a fancy to Halcyon and was usually waiting in the yard to greet her when she arrived for her ride and chattered volubly while Jules brought out her mount and gave her a leg up into the saddle. When she was a big lady, she informed Halcyon, in a mixture of French and English, she too would ride a big horse and gallop across the pasture field, but *hélas*, she was still so small she could only manage the Shetland pony, which was too lazy to gallop, and she was growing too big for it.

'We shall have to ask the Seigneur to procure another pony for you, *mon petit chou*,' Jules said indulgently.

'I don't want a pony, I want *un cheval*, as big as Mademoiselle's.'

'*Bien*, not quite. Mademoiselle is a few sizes larger than you are, *ma petite*.'

Suzanne stamped her foot pettishly. 'I want a horse!'

'Will Monsieur de Valprès buy another pony for her?' Halcyon asked as Jules assisted her to mount.

'*Mais oui*, mademoiselle. He adores the little one and always spoils her.'

'Lucky Suzanne,' Halcyon laughed with an odd little pain at her heart. Raoul must be as fond of children as she was, but she had an idea Mariette did not care for them.

Some ten days after she had come to Bellevue, during which time she never saw Raoul, she came a little earlier than usual to the stables, actually before sunrise. It was almost cool, a pearly mist covered the distant river, out of which the twin towers of the Chateau des Saules stuck up like rocks in a calm sea; a hushed expectancy lay over the land waiting for the appearance of the sun, and the scorched grass beneath her feet was damp with the dew that all too soon would evaporate.

A high wooden palisade divided the chalet from the stables, which was overhung with climbing roses, red, white and pink cascades of bloom that filled the air with fragrance. Halcyon paused and gazed at it, wondering if Raoul was awake in the small house it enclosed. He must know that it was at this hour she took her exercise and that was why he was never visible. She sighed wistfully, and continued her way into the stable yard. This was square with loose-boxes and buildings all round it and a stone water trough in the middle. Standing by it she saw to her astonishment Raoul de Valprès, who had obviously just returned from a morning gallop, for Saracen was covered with lather which lay in white streaks on his black satin coat. Raoul was wearing the riding gear that so became him, well cut breeches and polished boots with a mesh yellow tee shirt open at the neck. He looked spruce, lean and lithe, his face burned almost to the colour of teak, his bare black head shining like a raven's wing. Jules and Suzanne were standing beside him and as Halcyon came into the yard, he lifted the little girl on to Saracen's back and she chuckled with glee.

'Make him gallop!' she cried, shaking the reins.

'*Mon Dieu*, not on Saracen, my little Amazon,' Raoul exclaimed. 'Hasn't she got a pony, Jules? What does she ride?'

'The Shetland, monsieur, but he grows too fat and she grows too big—it was about that I wished to speak to you.'

'Get something more suitable for her. Welsh ponies are good,' Raoul told him carelessly. 'Hold tight, Suzy.' He began to lead Saracen round the yard. Suzanne looked minute perched on the great horse's back, but she was not in the least alarmed.

'Make him trot,' she commanded.

Raoul obediently urged the beast forward, running to keep pace with it. Halcyon flattened herself against the wall to give them passage as they came towards her, but when he caught sight of her, Raoul instantly brought the animal to a halt. She was looking very slim and trim in jodhpurs and shirt, a felt hat shielding eyes and nape, but his glance was critical and disparaging. Halcyon felt a cold trickle run down her spine as his face hardened to granite. She would not have believed tawny eyes could look so glacial. It was obvious that he resented her presence, the easy familiarity he had shown towards Suzanne had vanished to be replaced with something very like antagonism.

Discouraged, she turned away with the intention of leaving the yard, she could not bear to remain under his displeasure.

Jules spoke from behind him.

'I will have your mare ready in five minutes, mademoiselle.'

'You are going out?' Raoul asked coldly.

'Madame de Valprès arranged that I should ride at this hour.' Somehow she managed to get the words out though she had a choking sensation in her throat. She had wished to see Raoul so much, and now she had met him, he was rejecting her. 'You ... you don't object?' she faltered.

'Why should I object?'

'I don't know. I thought you were displeased.'

But now he had recovered the poise her unexpected appearance had shaken, his annoyance masked, and he smiled, a smile Halcyon was sure was forced.

'How could I be displeased that you have found some recreation?' he asked. 'It seems to me you work much too hard. Every night I hear the clack of your typewriter.' His smile became mocking. 'While you direct the course of true love. What a pity real life is so contrary and cannot be guided into the right channels to ensure the happy ending.'

Halcyon glanced at him uncertainly, wondering if he were implying that he had reached a stalemate with

Mariette, but she knew he was not guided by love in that direction. She caught the mischievous gleam in his half-closed eyes and realised he was merely laughing at her and her literary efforts.

Before she could think up a sufficiently scathing retort, Suzanne created a diversion. She had become impatient with their, to her, incomprehensible dialogue. She kicked Saracen's flank and though her small heels could make little impression upon his glossy hide, he threw up his head and began to dance. Raoul's attention was detached from Halcyon as he endeavoured to quiet the big horse, while Suzanne laughed gleefully. Then Jules appeared leading the quiet bay mare that had been allotted for Halcyon's use.

'You ride alone?' Raoul asked as she went forward to take the reins.

'I believe Jules usually hovers around,' she returned, smiling at the little man, for though the groom did not officially escort her she frequently noticed him following her at a distance.

'Mademoiselle is an expert horseman,' Jules declared, 'but even so the unforeseen accident can occur. I merely keep one eye open for her while I exercise the other horses.'

'I am glad you do,' Raoul approved as Halcyon put her foot into the stirrup and swung herself easily into the saddle. Jules handed her the crop she hardly ever used, and stood back. She raised it in valediction to Raoul.

'*Au 'voir*, Monsieur de Valprès.'

The formal nomenclature made him frown. Perverse creature, Halcyon thought, what else can he expect after the way he looked at me?

'My horse is bigger than yours,' Suzanne called triumphantly, as Halcyon rode past her.

'Much bigger. 'Bye, *chérie*!'

The mare broke into a trot when she was through the gateway. Halcyon heard a squeal of protest from the yard which indicated that Suzanne had been forcibly dismounted. She smiled as she guided the mare across the pasture field towards the woods. It was good of Raoul to indulge the little monkey, but his patience was not infinite. She had never seen him with a child before, it was a new aspect of him. Naturally he would want a family to come after him at the chateau, and it seemed he would be an indulgent parent.

She checked the mare to a walk as she reviewed the incident that had just taken place. Raoul's expression when he had noticed her had given her a shock. It had brought home to her how low she had fallen in his estimation, and all because of that wretched episode with Louis. Once on that never-to-be-forgotten night, he had asked her not to misjudge his actions, but he had not extended the same tolerance to her. To be fair, she supposed that if she had caught him with a girl in his arms other than Mariette, she would have arrived at and the same conclusion that he had done. But perhaps with more justification since he was credited with many affairs by uncharitable gossips. Still, a break had had to come, Louis or no Louis, now he was seriously wooing Mariette, and she, Halcyon, was quite sure would not be tolerant.

Reminded of the other girl, she looked towards the chateau. The sun was coming up from below the horizon and its beams were dispersing the mist that lay over the river. The chateau was emerging from its enshrouding veil, an impressive pile, but only a building. Rootless herself, it was difficult for her to understand how its grey stones could be worth the sacrifice of personal happiness, which Raoul was unlikely to find in such a disparate union, but of course she was looking at the matter from the wrong angle. Frenchmen did not marry for happiness but for a dowry.

The edge of the wood came nearer, its depths looking cool and inviting. There was a ride through it that she often followed, which rose slightly through the trees to a hill top from whence there was an even finer view. She glanced behind her, wondering if the faithful Jules would be hovering, as she had put it, in her rear. She suspected that Madame de Valprès had instructed him to keep her within sight. Sure enough a horse and rider was crossing the field towards her. Suddenly she went tense. It was not Jules' small crouched figure on the back of the chestnut stallion which she knew was the pride of the stable and fleeter even than Saracen, but a tall lean figure that was only too familiar. Moroever, he made no pretence of hovering, but was coming towards her at a canter, evidently determined to overtake her. Halcyon wondered vaguely what could be his purpose, was she going where she should not trespass? But she had often ridden in the wood before. Recalling the coldness of his greeting, she felt a flick of resentment. She was not going to allow him to order her to return on the plea that she had overstepped her privileges, she would not stay to listen to him. Gathering up her reins, she urged the mare to a gallop.

As she passed into the wood, a twist in the ride obscured her pursuer, if he were pursuing her. Checking her pace, she listened, but could hear no beat of hooves on the soft ground. Fool, she thought, her cheeks flushing, he was only exercising the stallion, and he had no intention of catching me up. But there had been purpose in that galloping figure and when a twig snapped and the mare whinnied, she knew she was wrong, and he was still following her.

Urged forward by some atavistic instinct, that of the quarry to escape capture, Halcyon increased her pace recklessly, reckless because the woodland glade was a place for caution. Low branches could sweep an unwary equestrian from the saddle, and there were stretches where the ground was wet and spongy. There were definite sounds behind her now to indicate that she was being chased—once Raoul called to her to stop with urgency in his voice, but she did not heed him and for the first time used her crop. The mare plunged forward at the unexpected blow, throwing up a cloud of mud in her wake. A bird, possibly a pheasant—the de Valprès had once reared them—flew across the path ahead of her uttering a harsh cry. The mare shied violently, swung aside under the low branch of an oak, which struck Halcyon on the head, and as she slipped from her saddle, the green foliage, the filtered sunlight were blotted out.

'Don't!' Someone was trying to force liquid between her lips. Weakly she endeavoured to brush away the hand that held it.

'It is only water,' someone said, and with an effort she opened her eyes. The green and gold of the forest shimmered before her vision, and as her sight cleared, she became aware that she was lying on a bed of moss and fallen leaves, and Raoul was kneeling beside her, one hand behind her head, while he held a cup of water to her lips. Abruptly she sat up.

'What happened?'

'You fell off your horse.'

He sat back on his haunches and emptied the water from the cup on to the leaves; it was the top of a flask, and he carefully screwed it back into place.

'Luckily there was a flask of water in my saddle bag,

and another of something stronger, left over from some expedition, but I know better than to offer you spirits until we have ascertained the damage.'

He spoke almost at random, to disguise acute anxiety, and Halcyon did not take in his words. Dazedly she looked around. The chestnut was tied to a nearby tree, but of the bay mare there was no sign. Raoul was replacing the flask in his saddle holster, and unsteadily she struggled to her feet, feeling peeved that he had not stayed to help her. But naturally he would be annoyed with her for running away. Why had she? She did not know except that she had had a sensation of being hunted. She put her hand to her forehead and gingerly touched the bruise that had formed.

'Apparently there are no bones broken, and it was entirely your own fault.' Raoul's voice was curt and cold. 'Whatever possessed you to ride at that pace through the trees?'

'Whatever possessed you to come after me?' she returned. She dropped her eyes as she saw his wry smile. 'You did, you know.'

'And so you fled—why?'

'I don't know . . .'

'Am I so hateful to you?'

A purely rhetorical question, he must know very well he was not.

She sniffed and felt for her handkerchief.

'You . . . you've avoided me ever since I came here,' she accused him, and blew her nose, wishing she did not feel so near to tears. Had she been less shaken she would not have mentioned the matter of his avoidance, for which he had reasons, but it had been very much upon her mind, and she blurted it out without thinking.

'I had to.' Then something seemed to snap inside

him. In one swift movement he was beside her and they were in each other's arms. He held her fiercely, possessively, almost brutally, crushing her hard against his lean muscular body, while his mouth devoured her face and neck. With his lips against her ear, he began to speak angrily, desperately:

'*Imbécile*, little idiot, why did you do it? For a moment I thought you were dead—you looked so white.' His hold became cruelly close. 'That was the last thing I would wish. Oh, damn you, 'Alcyone, why must you always come between me and my carefully conceived plans? You have caused far too many complications.'

She could make no answer to these accusations, for his mouth closed over hers. Still shaken by her fall, her senses overwhelmed by his embrace, she could not assimilate what he had said. A surge of passionate emotion, as strong as his, submerged her. Her body became fluid in his grasp, her lips responded to his. She felt herself sinking deep into a well of sensuality, and all that mattered was that he should continue to make love to her, until she found she was flat on a couch of pine needles and his weight was pinning her down.

'No,' she gasped, wrenching her face away from his. 'Not like this!'

'How else, *mignonne*?' His voice was a thick murmur.

Realisation came flooding back and with it some measure of sanity. Her instinct had been right when it had urged her to flee him. He had said he wanted everything from her but the one essential, and now he was about to take all—without love. But she was not prepared to give. He belonged to another woman and the weakness of her surrender had led him to believe he could have his way with her and go back to Mariette without compunction. She was of no account, the poor artist's daughter, and he was treating her with no more consideration than his ancestors had shown when they claimed the *droit du seigneur* from the poor brides of their peasantry. A fierce pride awoke in her; this was not love, it was raw primitive passion, and coupled with pride was fear.

'No,' she cried again, then wildly. 'No, never!'

'But, *chérie* ...'

He rolled to one side, but his hands were still on her body, caressing hands, well practised hands—*well practised*; she was by no means the first.

With all her strength she drew away from him and managed to regain her feet. He lay on his back, looking up at her, his eyes glittering slits between his half-closed lids with their fringes of thick lashes.

'What are you afraid of?' he asked languidly. 'You know you want to.'

'No, I don't.' She pushed her disordered hair out of her eyes. 'I will not be seduced like ... like one of your peasant girls out for a frolic!'

'You must not malign them,' he murmured lazily. 'The girls of Gracedieu are very well behaved, except perhaps at vintage time. Is that what you are waiting for, my little Bacchante, the madness of the grape? But vintage time is some way off and we are here alone now.'

She drew back, fighting with an urge to throw herself down beside him.

'Since you are so fond of classical allusions,' she said in a stifled voice, 'Vestal Virgin would be more appropriate.'

'What?' Consternation brought his eyes wide open. He sat up and stared at her. Halcyon met his gaze bravely, though hot colour stained her face. Her eyes had gone dark in her pale face, which held no hint of coquetry. She looked as she had hinted, virginal.

'*Mon Dieu*, what a brute you must think I am!' Raoul exclaimed. 'But you misled me. You belong to the artists' fraternity which I know is unconventional. You are British and the British boast of their permissive society. Oh, yes, I have wondered about you, been puzzled too. You seemed so candid and innocent, though a little provocative at times.' He smiled reminiscently. 'But when I found you in that drop-out's arms, I decided the innocence was a clever act and you could not be at all particular.'

'Oh, but I am,' Halcyon exclaimed, shocked to discover the reason for Raoul's contempt. 'You don't know how thankful I was when you came in. Louis had just asked me to marry him. Yes, Raoul, I said marry,' for the Frenchman had raised his eyebrows. 'He was prepared to reform for my sake, go into his father's office—the Perrons are quite substantial people really, but I ... I had to refuse. He wouldn't believe that I meant it and he ... he became a bit violent. He was jealous of you ... I don't know why,' she interpolated quickly as a quick gleam of triumph showed in Raoul's eyes. 'So when he saw you he tried to make out I ... I'd encouraged him. To salve his wounded vanity, I suppose. But it wasn't true. I always found him a bit of a nuisance, but I was sorry for him ... in a way ...'

She broke off and began to dig with the toe of her boot into a patch of soft moss, wondering if Raoul believed her story.

'I ... I've wanted to explain ever since,' she added, 'but you never gave me a chance.'

In the pause that followed, some bird in the undergrowth began to twitter, and the jingle of the chestnut's bit was audible as the horse pulled at the tether-

133

ing reins. Throughout her recital, Raoul's eyes had never left Halcyon's face, and her sincerity was obvious. At length as she stood with drooping head, staring at the moss, he said quietly:

'I have done you an injustice, 'Alcyone, but it changes nothing.' With a quick lithe movement he gained his feet, and instinctively, she moved a little further away from him.

'Why should it?' she asked, 'except that now you won't think so badly of me, will you?'

He seemed about to speak, hesitated, then said explosively:

'You should not go about unchaperoned, and your father does not care what you do. He leaves you unprotected.'

'Oh, Raoul, I'm not a Victorian miss,' she protested. 'Modern girls know how to look after themselves.'

Raoul laughed. 'You do not seem to be very good at it. How many times have I had to rescue you, including today?'

'I'd have been all right if you hadn't come after me,' she said reproachfully.

'So I am always to blame?' He leaned negligently against the bole of a tree. 'But I am not going to apologise. You may boast of your modern freedom, but from my point of view girls like you are a menace. You go about oozing provocation and when men accept your challenge you turn into marble pillars of outraged virtue. The first time I saw you you had practically nothing on.'

'You shouldn't have been there.'

'Then you had to go and puncture your foot.'

'That was a genuine accident, I couldn't help it.'

'Followed by inviting me to dinner in your private rooms.'

'I didn't invite you. It was your own idea.'

'You deliberately tantalised me in another man's arms.'

'Oh, really, Raoul, what is all this? You know you came quite unexpectedly and I've explained...'

Unheeding, he interrupted:

'Finally you have to bolt from me as if I were Lucifer's self.'

'I'll admit that was foolish...'

'At last you admit something. *Eh bien,* I suppose you cannot help being a maddening little witch.'

'I'm no such thing, and in case you're thinking of adding it to your list of provoking actions, or whatever you term them, I would like you to know I came to Bellevue at your mother's urgent request with some idea of paying back a little of my debts to you.'

'You owe me nothing,' he said quickly, 'and as for Maman ...' a curious expression crossed his face. 'I was not consulted about your appointment as her secretary. My mother is a very devious woman, I suspect she may have foreseen what happened today.'

Halcyon gaped at him. 'How could she?'

Raoul said solemnly, 'She is a clever student of human nature. *Alors,* I have circumvented her so far, and...' He paused and glanced at her uncertainly. 'I shall continue to do so,' he concluded, but he sounded more as if he were trying to convince himself than her.

'What are you talking about?' Halcyon asked doubtfully.

He regarded her quizzically. 'You don't know? *Bon,* I hoped you were not a party to her schemes. *Eh bien,* we should be returning.'

'Unfortunately I've lost my mount.'

'Which fortunately is the only thing you have lost,' he told her with such intention that Halcyon blushed fierily. 'The mare will have gone home and Jules will be wondering what has happened to you.'

'Then you'd better ride on ahead and tell him I'm on my way,' Halcyon told him quickly, fearful that he might propose that they rode together. Her nerves were still raw and quivering and she could not bear further contact with him.

'You shall ride,' he informed her, untying the stallion's reins. 'And I will lead him. You could not control him if I did not.'

'I don't mind walking, it isn't far.'

'Quite a step, and you have had a fall.' With a flash of imperiousness, he added, 'Will you do as you are told, or must I make you?'

'Oh, very well.'

She had to submit to his aid to mount the tall horse. When she was in the saddle, he brushed some of the mud from her jodhpurs with his hands, saying drily: 'The fall will account for your dishevelled appearance, which is not entirely due to it.'

She laughed nervously, at his allusion which turned to genuine amusement as she suddenly realised what a spectacle they presented. Both were plentifully bedaubed with mud and pine needles.

'How will you account for your appearance?' she enquired mischievously.

'I won't have to. I can change before anyone sees me, but you will have to go back to Bellevue, unless you would like to take advantage of my chalet's amenities to clean up?'

He had taken hold of the stallion's bridle and was leading the snorting animal down the woodland path. The beast did not approve of its change of riders. At mention of his house, Raoul shot a wicked glance at her over his shoulder. Halcyon would very much like to have seen its interior, the place where he spent his days, but knew, that she dared not follow up his suggestion.

'No, thank you. If I accept that would only be added to your list of provocations.'

'So you are learning correctitude? I am not sure I do not prefer your indiscretions.'

Looking straight between the chestnut's ears at the winding path ahead, she said coldly:

'They were quite unintentional, and there will be no more of them.'

'You speak with certainty.' Again that wicked look up at her. 'Can you control your own impulsive nature ... and destiny?'

'If need be.' Seeking a safer topic, she went on: 'I didn't realise you were so fond of children. Suzanne is a dear little thing.'

'Why should I not be fond of children?' he asked indignantly. 'I am not a monster. Some day I hope to have a family.'

Mariette's babies, Halcyon thought with a pang, the heirs to the Chateau des Saules.

'They'll be in rather a different position from Suzanne,' she observed. 'I expect your wife will employ nurses.'

'Possibly, but I shall reserve to myself the pleasure of teaching them to ride.' He smiled almost tenderly. 'My sons must be good horsemen.'

'They'll probably prefer sports cars.'

'Not if they are true de Valprès.'

They had come out into the pastures field and the chateau was visible in the valley illuminated by the early sunlight. Raoul looked towards it and sighed.

A little nettled, because she knew his thoughts had gone from her to his ancestral home, Halcyon said:

'I find it a little difficult to understand how mortar and stones can be worth so much to you.'

'For a historical novelist you seem surprisingly devoid of imagination,' he retorted. 'I belong where my ancestors were.'

Halcyon looked down upon the proudly held black head, today he wore no hat. Every inch of him proclaimed his aristocratic blood, but she was sure he was making a disastrous mistake by contracting this loveless marriage, and she had a sudden suspicion that his mother thought so too—but then Cécile had not been born a de Valprès.

CHAPTER EIGHT

As a result of her misadventure, Halcyon was late for *petit déjeuner* at Bellevue. Madame de Valprès was already seated in the patio, when after a hurried shower, Halcyon joined her, having put on a clean dress and arranged her hair over her forehead to conceal the darkening bruise.

She had left Raoul at the stables, insisting that she was sufficiently recovered to walk the short distance alone. She needed time to recover her equilibrium before facing her employer. Raoul's half jesting, half bitter comments upon her conduct had been illuminating, betraying as they did how strongly he resented the attraction that she seemed to have for him. But her conscience was clear. She had never deliberately encouraged his advances, believing that he meant to marry Mariette. Apparently he still did, and she almost wished he would get himself married and simplify her position. Almost, for she was sure he would be laying up unhappiness for himself in the days to come, and she cherished a faint hope that something would happen to prevent the union.

The breakfast café-au-lait was always served French fashion in little bowls, the beans being freshly ground every morning. Madame was very particular about her coffee, and its making was almost a ritual. As the girl slipped into her seat, Cécile looked up with a frown.

'You are late and your coffee is cold,' she told her,

ringing the handbell on the table beside her. 'You know Clothilde dislikes being asked to warm it up—besides, it is never so good.'

'I don't mind drinking it tepid,' Halcyon said hastily, anxious not to give trouble, but Clothilde had already appeared and took away the offending beverage with a droop of her sulky underlip.

Madame had the morning's mail beside her on another table. It was her habit to run through it at the conclusion of her meal before handing it over to Halcyon to deal with, extracting anything personal. The bulk of it Halcyon would take into the room which Madame called alternatively her office, her study or even the library, for there were many books on shelves in it. There a much more imposing typewriter than her own little portable was designated for her use.

Halcyon apologised for her tardiness, explaining that she had had a fall, and Cécile's manner became more sympathetic.

'*Tiens, quel malheur!*' she exclaimed. 'It has shaken you, has it not?' For Halcyon was pale, less the result of her accident than the emotional scene through which she had passed. 'But how did it happen? Where was Jules?'

Somewhat unwillingly, Halcyon gave her an expurgated account of the morning's happenings, saying that her horse had bolted into the wood, and Raoul had succoured her. There was no point in suppressing that information, as he would in all probability tell his mother of the incident when he met her at dinner, though she was reluctant to mention him, fearing she might betray too much to the elder woman's keen eyes.

Clothilde brought back the reheated bowl of coffee, while Madame regarded her young protégée with a little knowing smile. Halcyon drank it gratefully, while an uneasy suspicion stirred in her that her hostess knew a great deal more about her relations with her son than she had supposed.

'So Raoul was your knight errant,' Cécile de Valprès said thoughtfully. 'But why didn't he return with you? You must have needed his support.'

'I was quite all right by the time I got back to the stables, only a bit muddy, the ground was so damp.' To her dismay she felt herself blush at the memory of what had transpired upon that damp ground. She broke a croissant with nervous fingers though she was not hungry, wishing Madame de Valprès would not study her with that penetrating stare. To divert her, she asked if there was anything urgent in the post.

'No, and I think I must excuse you this morning, you do not look fit to work.'

'Really, madame, I'm feeling fine now,' Halcyon protested.

'I don't think you are, and you are very pale except when I speak of Raoul.' She smiled at the girl's embarrassed look. Turning her gaze away from her, she looked across the pool to the potted cypresses against the further wall, and said deliberately:

'My son cannot make up his mind, but it is possible Mademoiselle Dubois may force his hand. She grows tired of waiting for him to declare himself.'

Halcyon stared at her in surprise.

'But ... but I thought it was all settled.'

'It should have been on the night of the ball. Papa was all set to make the announcement.' Her eyes came back to Halcyon with a mischievous twinkle in their dark depths. 'But the prospective bridegroom had disappeared. Perhaps you know what happened to him?'

Halcyon took a gulp of her coffee and nearly choked. Recovering herself, she said guardedly:

'Why should you think that?'

'I am not blind, *ma chère*. I saw his face when he was dancing with you. Of course in the old days there would have been no problem. Then Monsieur married as arranged and took a mistress, or perhaps he already had one. Madame, once the succession was secured, was allowed a lover, providing she was discreet. So everyone was happy, but now...' She shrugged her shoulders.

Halcyon did not say anything, but her expression was disdainful. She would never take second place to Mariette even to make Raoul happy, if that was what Madame was implying.

'*Eh bien,*' Madame went on, 'the old traditions are dead, but I think my son is making a big mistake in sacrificing his happiness to his desire to own the chateau. It has become an obsession with him, and he loathes seeing the Dubois in possession.'

'So you don't approve of his marriage to Mariette?' Halcyon asked, realising that her sudden suspicion had been correct.

'I do not, but he will not listen to me. It is true that he promised his father ... perhaps I should explain. You may have heard that the de Valprès emigrated to Canada?' Halcyon nodded. 'They prospered there, but they always had a yearning for the old country. My husband came over to fight in the last war, and when it was over he decided to settle here and bought Belle-vue. That was when he married me.' The thin aristo-cratic face softened. 'We were ideally happy, it was *not* an arranged marriage—that is until he began to fret about the chateau. It had been used as a hospital under the Vichy Government, and he was hoping it would eventually be released, and he could snap it up, to which end he saved all his resources. But they had far more important matters to settle than the fate of the Chateau des Saules, and before it came on the market Etienne died.' Madame paused, and her eyes misted. 'He was too young to die, but his wartime experiences had undermined his health.'

Halcyon looked down at her plate, unwilling to intrude upon an old grief. Cécile sniffed, wiped her eyes and continued, 'Raoul loved his father. He was only a lad when Etienne died. and when he was—my husband, I mean—on his deathbed, he made Raoul promise to do everything in his power to get the Chateau des Saules back for the family. and my son took it as a sacred trust. He was at an impressionable age.'

Madame became silent, fingering her letters, then she went on briskly:

'*Eh bien*, the chateau never was put up for sale. Dubois was in the know and obtained it cheap. Raoul was furious, until he realised that Mariette offered an easy way for him to keep his promise.'

Halcyon moved a little impatiently. All this talk of deathbed promises and sentimental attachment to a pile of stones seemed to her to be a little absurd. Raoul had a pleasant and compatible life at Bellevue without involving himself with an uncongenial mate. Etienne de Valprès, she decided, must have been unbalanced by the war and the promise he had extracted from his young son was unfair.

'You haven't the same regard for the Chateau des Saules yourself, madame?' she hazarded.

'Certainly not. Bellevue is good enough for me. We have built the place up with our own efforts and it is more to be proud of than that ancient monument, even if it is the cradle of the original de Valprès.' She looked at Halcyon intently. 'I am relying upon you to break Raoul's obsession with it.'

'Me?' Halcyon was startled. 'But, madame, what can I do?'

'You are in love with him, *n'est-ce pas?*'

'Oh, madame, is it so obvious?' Halcyon cried aghast.

Cécile smiled. 'Be easy, child, he is not aware of it.'

Halcyon was not sure of that. This morning in his arms, her emotional response must have told him that she was far from indifferent to him, but now he knew she was a virtuous woman, she anticipated that he would not expose her to further temptation.

'He is more than half in love with you,' Madame went on, but Halcyon shook her head.

'That can't be. He has avoided me all the time I've been here.'

'Because he fears you may divert him from his purpose, as you did at the ball.'

'I had no intention of doing that. I don't deny there's some sort of physical attraction between us, but he doesn't love me.'

'You're splitting hairs,' Madame said calmly. She leaned towards Halcyon across the table, and told her earnestly:

'You could get him away from Mariette if you tried.'

'I don't think so.' Halcyon covered her face with her hands. 'I ... I'm not permissive, madame.'

'I know that. You are the sort of girl I would like my son to marry.'

Halcyon looked up. 'But I'm a nobody—I've no *dot*.'

'There is plenty here for all of us, provided Raoul does not waste our substance by paying an impossible price for the chateau. I believe you could make Raoul happy, if you tried.'

Halcyon looked at her hostess directly with clear, candid eyes.

'I daren't make any overtures to your son, they

would only end one way. This morning, in the wood, he nearly seduced me.'

Colour flamed in her pale cheeks as she made this admission, but she must persuade her hostess that contact with Raoul was too dangerous.

'You mean you resisted him?' Cécile asked. 'Was not that a little foolish?'

'But, madame...' Halcyon began to expostulate.

'You should have allowed him to bring matters to a head,' Madame said regretfully. Then seeing the shocked surprise in the girl's eyes, she explained: 'Raoul is honourable. If his hot blood overcame him, he would make amends to you in the only possible way, and that would settle Mariette.'

Raoul had said his mother was a devious woman, and Halcyon began to see what he meant. Madame de Valprès was determined to detach him from Mariette, or more correctly the chateau, and she was not scrupulous how she did it. Halcyon now suspected that her secretarial engagement had been part of her plan. Cécile knew that sooner or later she must meet Raoul, and what had happened that morning was much what she had anticipated.

She said very quietly, 'It wouldn't do, madame. Raoul would hold it against me ever afterwards that I had tricked him into marriage and come between him and his dream. Only this morning he told me he belonged where his ancestors had been.'

'He is trying to convince himself he does, and not, I fancy, very successfully,' Cécile said drily. 'He would be grateful to you for solving his dilemma.'

'He must do that for himself,' Halcyon insisted, 'and there's nothing I can do to help him.'

'*Tiens*, of course there is. If only you would overcome that maidenly reserve of yours, which is a bit of an anachronism in this day and age.'

'What precisely do you want me to do?' Halcyon asked bluntly.

'Let your heart speak.'

Halcyon recalled Raoul's mocking accusations of provocation, and shook her head.

'He doesn't want my heart.'

'He does not know what he does want, and it is up to you to show him.'

Halcyon thought Madame was wrong there. Raoul wanted the chateau and herself, but he put the chateau a long way first.

'He'll keep out of my way in future,' she observed despondently.

'Then you must be put in his. Tonight you will dine with us.'

'Oh, madame . . .'

'Looking beautiful, and you could look beautiful properly dressed.'

'Please, madame . . .'

'*Ecoutez.*' Cécile de Valprès talked fast and eagerly, outlining her plan, while Halcyon listened, alternatively flushing and paling. Somewhat unwillingly she agreed to the first part of the procedure. The temptation to dine with Raoul, for once well dressed—Madame had said she would lend her a dress—was too much for her. Except for the time when she had worn the Empire gown, and that had been a home-made affair in cheap muslin, he had always encountered her in anything but glamorous clothes, and she knew that she could look good if she were dressed up.

Regarding what was to follow that depended upon Raoul's reactions and about those she was not nearly so sanguine as his mother was. She could hold her own against Mariette, for whatever his feelings were to-

146

wards herself, he had expressed nothing but indifference towards his prospective bride, but Mariette plus the Chateau des Saules was another proposition. Only a deep and genuine emotion could wean him from his obsession with the place, and she was certain that all she was to him was a passing fancy that he had believed to be available until she had confessed her innocence. That he had ever thought her to be otherwise, before the Louis episode, she doubted. He was adept at gallantry and pretty speeches. But her admission had shaken him and whatever his faults he appeared to respect virtue, so that she anticipated that he would keep his distance in future.

But there was no harm in dressing up and meeting him for dinner with his mother, and Madame could see for herself when they met how impossible was the course she had suggested.

When evening approached, Halcyon was feeling quite herself again after a restful day. Even the bruise upon her forehead seemed to be fading. She put on the evening dress Cécile had lent her, for she did not possess one of her own. It was of soft white crêpe, and since she and Madame de Valprès were much of a size, it had only needed taking in at the waist. It fell in graceful folds to her feet, and the bodice with its tiny sleeves had a cowl neckline. It was both virginal and provocative, for though it appeared so demure, it clung to the lines of her body when she moved. It had been cut by a master couturier, who knew his business, and Halcyon revelled in its lovely lines, feeling sure it was the first and last time she would ever wear such a garment.

She made up carefully, using green eye-shadow which turned her hazel eyes to emeralds. Her hair she did as she had worn it for the ball, piled up on her head, with one long lock falling upon her shoulder, which she curled to form a ringlet. Her whole appearance was a little similar to the Empire style she had worn upon that occasion, though the waistline was normal and fine crêpe was infinitely superior to muslin. She had no jewellery, except the gold locket, which must serve again.

'I'm not sure,' she apostrophised her image in the glass, 'whether I'm a lamb being led to the slaughter or a siren bent upon seduction!' and laughed a little breathlessly. Whatever happened she did not anticipate that her evening would be dull.

Raoul was already present when she came into Madame's sitting room. This was in front of the house, with tall windows looking out on to the garden. There was nothing Spanish about its furnishings, it was entirely French, with mirrors and candle sconces upon its panelled walls, and ornate furniture, its only concession to comfort being a large modern settee.

If he was surprised to see her, he concealed it, but his eyes were jewel-hard, with the glitter of yellow topaz as he surveyed her. She gained the impression that he was displeased, but he said politely:

'An unexpected pleasure.'

'I thought it would be a change for Halcyon to dine with us,' Cécile explained casually. 'She is too much alone.'

'If she is, I am sure that is her own choice,' Raoul remarked gallantly.

Halcyon wondered whom he thought there was at Bellevue to relieve her solitude, but suspected it was merely a *façon de parler*.

'Dinner is ready for us,' Madame de Valprès said, and her son offered her his arm. 'No, you must escort our guest,' she declared, laughing. 'I will precede you.'

Raoul dropped his arm and gave Halcyon a dark look. 'There's no need for ceremony when we are *en famille*,' he observed.

Madame smiled at him over her shoulder. 'Yes, Halcyon is like one of the family now,' she said meaningly.

The *salle-à-manger*, across the hall and also facing to the front, was small but perfectly appointed, its pale tinted walls reflecting the golden gleam of candles on the oval table lit to augment the summer dusk. Halcyon was familiar with it as she lunched there with Cécile, but it seemed different tonight, more mellow and intimate in the soft lighting. Since Madame de Valprès liked ceremony at dinner time, Raoul wore a dinner jacket with a white shirt and black tie. His mother was wearing a décolleté gown in blue brocade. The village girl who waited upon them was a little inadequate in her duties and had to be prompted by her mistress.

'I am training her,' Cécile explained when the girl went out to change the courses. 'The last one left to go into a factory. I expect this one will too eventually.'

'Then isn't it rather wasted endeavour?' Raoul asked. 'We could wait upon ourselves.'

'I still cling to the habits of my youth,' his mother returned, 'though doubtless they will die with me.'

She looked at Halcyon enigmatically.

'Dubois employs footmen,' Raoul informed them.

'Now that I call ostentation,' Madame declared, 'but then, poor man, he has to try to be impressive, being so palpably *bourgeois*.'

'The *bourgeoisie* are in the ascendant,' Raoul said tersely. 'We aristocrats are out of date, Maman.'

'And so are footmen,' Cécile pointed out. 'It is absurd for Monsieur Dubois to try to ape the manners of a bygone age.'

'As you do, Maman,' Raoul gave her a sly smile.

'*Alors*, I was born to them. That is different.'

'Very different,' Raoul agreed.

Halcyon had made no contribution to this some-what aimless exchange, which appeared to be a covert way of sneering at Dubois, which she vaguely resented. Pierre Dubois was a kindly man, and deserved better appraisal from his arrogant son-in-law to be. Raoul was looking arrogant tonight, but whether his pride was affronted by the thought of the usurpers of his ancestral home or something else, she was not sure.

The conversation veered to the affairs of the estate, in which she could take little part, though Cécile occasionally threw her an explanation or asked her opinion. Raoul seemed determined to ignore her, addressing no remark to her, but his eyes continually rested upon her with the familiar sensuous sleepy look, which she now knew indicated desire. Her heart was beating uncomfortably fast and she wondered desperately what she was going to say to him when they were alone, for she did not doubt that Madame de Valprès would contrive to absent herself.

Sure enough, when they were back in the salon and had partaken of coffee, Madame made a pretext to leave them. She said vaguely that she would only be a few minutes, but Halcyon knew she would not return for some time.

She glanced uneasily at Raoul, who was lounging on the wide settee. Evening clothes became him; so dressed he looked the distinguished aristocrat, and immeasurably aloof from her. It was almost impossible to credit that he was the same man who had embraced her so fervently earlier in the day. Nor could the primitive atmosphere of the woods be compared with the sophistication of Madame's salon, the so very civilised furnishings demanded dignity and restraint.

'You ... you seem almost like a stranger tonight,' she said timidly, wishful to break a silence that was becoming oppressive.

'That is what you wish me to be, *n'est-ce pas*?' he returned repressively.

So she had been right when she had expected he would keep her at a distance after what had passed between them. Men like Raoul had nothing to say to the uninitiated, and she should be thankful that he had withdrawn his attentions, but with feminine lack of logic she resented his attitude. Seeking to break through his reserve, she asked appealingly:

'I would like us to be friends, surely there's no harm in that?'

'Friends!' She was surprised by his contemptuous tone. 'When have we ever been friends?'

'Oh, Raoul, that evening in the tower...' she began in bewilderment.

'You thought I was being friendly?' he cut in with infinite scorn in his glance.

'And all the other times,' she went on, 'until you found me with Louis. Raoul, how could you imagine I cared a damn for that drop-out?'

He smiled ruefully. 'I didn't, actually, but I tried to make myself believe so. I wanted to think you were a shallow, permissive little sensation-seeker, and that Louis Perron's oddity made him attractive to you.'

Halcyon felt a little surge of triumph, Raoul had forgotten to keep aloof. She said curiously:

'Why did you want to denigrate me?'

'It made it easier to fight my feelings for you.'

This admission was encouraging, implying as it did that he had been drawn to her as she had been to him.

Dropping her voice to a seductive murmur, she enquired:

'Why did you have to fight it, Raoul?'

Instantly his face hardened, his eyes were fossilised amber, as looking at her bleakly he demanded:

'Why are you dressed up in my mother's clothes? Aren't you devastating enough in your own?' He straightened his posture on the settee. 'She has put you up to this, *n'est-ce pas?*'

Halcyon blushed and hung her head, as she was thus reminded of Madame's injunctions. Did he suspect that his mother hoped to trap him through his emotions. She had not meant to try to rouse him, but had been unable to resist the lead he had given her when he confessed he was not indifferent, but now he showed no indication of softening towards her, he looked almost inimical. Pained by his animosity, she cried his name with infinite reproach:

'Oh, Raoul!'

'No more of that, *chérie*,' he said shortly. 'We are not in the woods now but in my mother's house, and I have recovered my sanity.'

She turned her head away, biting her lip, wishing she had not lowered her pride to ask for his friendship. He had seen through her manoeuvre and rejected her.

He glanced at her averted face, noting the delicate line of chin and throat, her skin like alabaster against the dark curtains behind her, the light from a wall bracket shining on her hair and turning it to dark flame. She was sitting on a low, high-backed chair, and the softly draped lines of her dress clung to her young lissom figure with unconscious seduction. The desolation in her pose betrayed how much he had hurt her.

He passed his hand over his dark head, rumpling

the well brushed hair, looked away and back again, finally demanding savagely:

'Why did you have to come here? I thought I was inured to folly!'

Surprised by his tone, she turned her head.

'Your mother asked me...' she began.

'I do not mean to Bellevue, I mean into my life. Disrupting it.'

He sprang to his feet and began to pace the room, thrusting his hands deep into his trouser pockets.

'No doubt Maman has told you that I promised my father that I would regain the chateau. He was deeply disappointed when Dubois acquired it, having saved all the money he made out of Bellevue towards its purchase. However, when it transpired that Dubois' only child was a girl, the way was easy. I met her in Paris and decided she could have been a lot worse, and it did not take me long to have the whole family eating out of my hand.' He lifted his head arrogantly. 'I could give them what all their money cannot buy, birth and breeding for their grandchildren. Had my father still been alive, he would no doubt have hurried on the wedding, but I was in no hurry to press my suit and forgo my freedom. But I procrastinated too long, for a green-eyed witch came to me through the willow trees and put a spell on me. Time and time again I tried to propose, but when the all-important question rose to my lips, I could not ask it, for you came between us.'

He came to a halt in front of her, and glared down at her.

'I tried to avoid you, but fate kept throwing us together. Then in the forest I thought, God forgive me, if you could tolerate that scrawny artist's embraces, why not mine, and I would get you out of my system, but when I expected to take a willing siren, I was rebuffed by a virginal lily.'

'Very nicely put!'

'*Bien*, I do not wish to sound indelicate, but you understand?'

'Oh, I understand you perfectly, but I'm neither a siren nor a lily, but a very ordinary girl.' She sighed, wishing she could either yield to him or put him out of her heart, but both actions were impossible. 'All you've been saying,' she went on, 'is illuminating, but not very complimentary either to me or Mariette, that is if you intend to marry her.'

She made herself speak quietly and coolly, though conflicting emotions were warring in her heart. She knew that at this point Madame de Valprès would expect her to throw herself into Raoul's arms and strive by physical contact to break down the defences he had erected between them, but pride and her natural fastidiousness restrained her. It was his part to woo, not hers, and all he was doing was inveigling against her. She glanced up at him furtively from under her lashes and saw a pulse was beating in his temple, his eyes were glittering and he wore an almost avid expression. He was in the grip of strong emotion, but there was no suggestion of tenderness, no hint of love.

'Do you want me to marry Mariette?' he asked abruptly.

Every nerve in her body was screaming 'No!' but she told him evenly:

'Since you set so much store by the chateau and you've given her expectations, I think you should.'

'That is not what I asked you.'

Her composure broke. 'Oh, Raoul,' she cried with anguish, 'that isn't for me to decide.' Her hand went to her throat. 'You hurt me.'

Satisfaction showed in his face. 'That is better,' he

said brutally. Swooping forward, he caught hold of her wrists and pulled her to her feet. Drawing her against himself, he whispered:

'*Chérie, mon ange, ma bien-aimée!*'

Now he was all beguiling charm. His voice was deep and tender as he murmured: 'I do not wish to hurt you, only to love you.'

'Love!' she exclaimed bitterly against his neck. 'Do you know what love is, Raoul?'

'This is near enough for me,' he returned thickly.

His hands moved down her back, pressing her against him. Emotion surged through her. But he had said he hoped that consummation would free him from his desire for her, or words to that effect. Even as she yielded to his fierce kisses, the words came back to her: 'Get you out of my system.' But she was too far gone to heed them, as sensation blotted out thought. He tore away the collar of her dress as his lips sought her throat, her neck, and below. Her bones seemed to turn to water in a grasp that was more cruel than kind. She felt him raise her in his arms and move towards the settee, and at the same time both became aware of a car stopping outside. That was unusual, for visitors rarely came to Bellevue after dark unless by invitation. The windows behind the silk curtains were open to the summer night and the hum of a car driven at speed had been audible for some time. Now they heard the door banged as its occupant alighted, and the loud pealing of the front door bell.

'*Morte de ma vie!*' Raoul muttered as his arms slackened. 'Who the devil can that be?' He allowed Halcyon to slide to her feet and both stood listening with a premonition of disaster.

Quick footsteps approached the door of the salon, which was flung open to reveal Mariette Dubois on the

155

threshold with Madame close behind her. The girl was in evening dress with a cloak flung over it. Her usually immaculate coiffure was dishevelled, her round face streaked with tears.

Raoul stared at her stupefied, while Halcyon hastily retreated into a corner, straightening her dress, and pulling the torn cowl into place.

Seeing Raoul, Mariette ran to him straight as a homing pigeon towards its loft, and flung her arms about him.

'Raoul, *mon ami*, you must come with me at once!'

Automatically Raoul's arms closed round the girl's body.

'What has happened, *ma petite*?' he asked gently, and Halcyon experienced a fierce throb of jealousy at the tender note in his voice. Was it his natural reaction to a creature in distress or was he much fonder of Mariette than he allowed?

Mariette began to sob. '*Mon père, il est malade,*' followed by a burst of weeping.

Somewhat incoherently she at last made herself clear. Pierre Dubois had had a heart attack. He was conscious but very ill, and he had asked for Raoul. Mariette had come in their car to fetch him.

'But why come to me?' Raoul asked doubtfully.

'To whom else?' Mariette asked surprised. 'Are you not *notre bon ami*? There is no other nearer than Paris, and Papa says he must speak with you. Oh, *mon cher, viens vite*, before it is too late!'

There was a second's tense pause, while Raoul mechanically stroked Mariette's dark head. Two pairs of eyes watched him anxiously, Halcyon's hazel and Madame's dark ones, and both sensed the thoughts churning in his mind. With Pierre Dubois ill, perhaps dying, he would be in command at the chateau until such time as Mariette made him its master. It was obvious why the sinking Dubois had sent for him—he wished to give his daughter and his property into his care, and if Raoul went with Mariette now he would be committed. He glanced at Halcyon, a veiled look which she could not interpret.

'*Eh bien, ma petite*, I will come,' he said at length. 'Your car waits? *Bon*, we will delay no longer.'

There was finality in that last sentence and Halcyon knew that she had been renounced. Dumbly she watched their exit, the tall man with his arm round Mariette's substantial waist, protectingly supporting her. They heard the car engine spring to life, and the soft purr of its powerful engine as it glided away.

Madame de Valprès gave Halcyon a wry look, noting as Mariette had not done the girl's torn dress and disordered hair.

'*Quel dommage*,' she exclaimed. 'Why could not Dubois have waited until morning to have his attack? Now all my work is undone!'

Repelled by the other's callousness, Halcyon remonstrated:

'Monsieur Dubois is very ill, madame, and his daughter much distressed.'

'And therefore holds a trump card. Raoul is always so soft with those in trouble. She will get him now.'

Halcyon made no rejoinder, though she winced inwardly. She looked down at the neck of her gown.

'I'm afraid your dress is torn, madame,' she said apologetically. 'Perhaps I can manage to mend it.'

Cécile laughed harshly. '*N'importe. Hélas*, this night has ended very differently from what I hoped!'

Halcyon felt unutterably weary. It had been a long day of continual emotional stress and she could bear no more.

'If you will excuse me, madame, I would like to go to bed.'

'Certainly, mademoiselle.' Cécile de Valprès voice was cold. Halcyon had failed to produce the desired result, and as the girl crept away she was unhappily aware that not only Raoul but his mother also had rejected her.

CHAPTER NINE

HALCYON slept late next morning and awoke too late to go for her ride. Not that she would have gone if she had been in time, for she did not feel equal to the exercise. She had passed a restless night, haunted by dreams of Raoul and Mariette. Lying on her bed from which she could see the sun-filled patio through the half-drawn curtains, she mentally reviewed the events of the previous day, turning hot with shame as she recalled how nearly she had allowed Raoul to ravish her, and that after he had been complaining that she was tempting him from his chosen path. Although he had gone with Mariette, she could not be sure that he would leave her alone in future, and it would be too humiliating to succumb to another woman's fiancé. She seemed to have some sort of fatal fascination for him that overcame his scruples when he was with her. An appeal to his baser nature, she assured herself, and that was not worthy of either of them. There was only one certain solution, she must leave Bellevue immediately and far away from its influences, endeavour to achieve some peace of mind.

Madame de Valprès greeted her coolly at breakfast. To Halcyon's enquiry for news of Monsieur Dubois, she shrugged her shoulders. Raoul had not returned; there would be time enough to learn what had happened when he did.

Halcyon for once had some mail—a letter from her

father, the first communication she had had from him since he left. Provence had come up to expectations and he and Louis were going on to the Camargue. He might return to Gracedieu in a month to six weeks' time, when he concluded, her engagement by the de Valprès would have ended. She also had a letter from her publisher enquiring about the progress of her next novel and enclosing a cheque for some foreign royalties. The amount was pleasantly sizeable and would serve to finance her plans. She would seek out some village in another department, lodge at some humble *auberge* and concentrate upon finishing her neglected story. By the time Felix was ready to come home, she would have finished it.

'So you wish to be away?' Madame observed, when Halcyon tentatively expressed her desire to leave her employ. '*Eh bien*, it is fortunate that my former secretary writes to tell me that she is more quickly recovered than was expected.' She gave Halcyon a shrewd look. 'You would prefer to be far away before my son's nuptials with Mariette are announced?'

Halcyon nodded. 'It is a great pity I ever came to Gracedieu,' she said, recalling Raoul's accusations. He had been well content with the Dubois alliance until she had unsettled him.

Madame gave one of her expressive Frnch shrugs.

'*C'est la vie.* I will not seek to detain you, *ma chère*. In fact as events have turned out, your presence here might be an embarrassment. I shall have to receive Mademoiselle Dubois and her mother. No, they have never visited here,' as Halcyon looked surprised. 'We French do not entertain much in our homes, and I have given them dinner at an hotel. But now I must invite them to come here.'

Halcyon saw her point. When Mariette came to

Bellevue, she might be suspicious of her presence there and be more perspicacious than she had been last night. It would be more comfortable for all concerned if she was not there. She stifled a little sigh; she liked Madame and had enjoyed the hospitality of her home, it was a little hard to be so summarily dismissed.

She decided to depart next morning on the first bus to Orléans, from whence she could get a train to any locality she fancied. She had not much luggage, the heaviest item being her typewriter. Raoul was absent all day. At lunch Madame informed her that he had rung up to say that Dubois was still critically ill and his wife and daughter needed his presence to sustain them, so he would stay at the chateau for the time being.

'I will inform him upon his return that urgent business called you away,' Cécile told her.

'I don't suppose my movements will be of any interest to Monsieur de Valprès,' Halcyon said a little bitterly.

'Men are predictable,' Madame observed, 'always they are excited by the creature that runs—the hunting instinct, *ma chère*, as old as time. You had better not tell me where you are going.'

'I don't know myself yet,' Halcyon remarked. The thought that Raoul might be tempted to pursue her was exciting but very improbable. He would have his hands too full with the chateau and Mariette to give her a thought. More probably he would be relieved that her disturbing presence had been removed.

In the late afternoon, when the day was cooler, she went to say goodbye to Jules Gissard and his family. The little man received her news with obvious regret.

'When you come not this morning I fear you were feeling some ill effects from your tumble,' he told her.

'And now you say you go away.'

Halcyon smiled wryly. The ill effects she had suffered from had not been the result of her fall, at least only indirectly. Jules was looking at her commiseratingly, for she was still very pale and there were dark marks under her eyes from her poor night. Today they were all hazel, the green light that flashed into them when she was animated obscured. Jules had deduced that there was something between her and his master, and though he admired and respected Raoul de Valprès, whom he knew to be courageous and honest, he knew little of his ways with women. He had heard that the Seigneur was courting Mademoiselle Dubois and wondered if that was what was distressing his companion. Too bad if her precipitate departure was to be laid at his master's door.

He insisted that she came into his small flat over the stabling where he said Madame Gissard would make her a cup of tea. That, he told her with a grin, was the *anglais'* usual panacea. Halcyon heroically drank the brew which his wife concocted that was unlike any tea she had ever tasted, reflecting that it was a pity Jules had not taught her how to make it.

Suzanne showed her her toys which were mostly horses. The child, her mother said, had never cared for dolls. Her greatest treasure was a skin-covered rocking horse, and when mounted upon it she would declare that she was winning La Grande Nationale.

'It is a lovely beast' Halcyon praised it. 'Black, like Saracen.' And felt a pang. Saracen and all he stood for now belonged to a past that she must forget.

'She insisted it must be black for that reason,' Jules explained. 'It was a Christmas present from the Seigneur. He is always most generous.'

'When I grow up I shall marry a man like the Seig-

162

neur,' suzanne announced.

'You fly high, *mignonne*,' Jules stroked her black curls. 'But who knows?'

Suzanne was devastated when she learned that Halcyon had come to say goodbye.

'But why, mademoiselle? Do not you like it here?'

'Very much, but it isn't my home as it is yours.'

'Could you not marry the Seigneur?' Suzanne suggested ingenuously. 'Then it would be.'

'Monsieur de Valprès is already engaged,' Halcyon said shortly.

Jules raised a sandy eyebrow.

'So,' he murmured, and sighed. 'We shall see little of him when he lives at the chateau.'

'His chalet will be to let,' Madame Gissard remarked thoughtfully. 'Perhaps he would lease it to us.' The flat was a little cramped and Madame was an opportunist.

'We do well enough here,' Jules told her gloomily. He was a man who disliked change.

'You will come back one day, mademoiselle?' Suzanne asked, eyeing Halcyon wistfully. 'You will have to see my new pony which is coming all the way from Wales.'

Halcyon smiled. 'Perhaps,' she said non-committally, though she knew very well she would not come that way again. She would have to return to Gracedieu to meet her father, but she intended to persuade him to move on immediately. That would not be difficult, for the summer would be nearly over and he preferred a town for winter quarters, but she would not want to come up to Bellevue, it held too many poignant memories.

It was time for Jules to feed his horses, and Halcyon took her leave. Suzanne clung to her at parting and she made vague promises to comfort her. The child would soon forget the English girl who had so briefly crossed her path.

When she had passed through the gateway into the yard, Halcyon paused before the rose-covered fence that surrounded Raoul's domain, the privacy of which she had never dared to invade. The owner was at the chateau and she felt an irresistible urge to view his home. She went along the fence until she came to a white wicket gate over which she could see the chalet, which was truly Swiss, with a deep-eaved roof and wooden balconies before the upstairs as well as the downstair windows. It looked deserted as the shutters were closed over them Madame Gissard would open them and make ready for his coming when advised of his return. His domestic chores were part of her duties. He must be lonely at times, Halcyon thought, but his mother was within easy reach and no doubt he liked to be independent.

In front of the house, in the middle of a smooth lawn, was a beautiful weeping willow. Intuition told her that it had been grown from a wand filched from those beside the Roman bath. She wondered who had planted it; it was too well grown to have been Raoul, it must have been his father, who had wished to perpetuate something from the chateau in his own domain.

Halcyon's eyes lingered on the tender green of the drooping wands. The tree was kept well watered, but even so some of the leaves were touched with yellow by the drought. A crown of willow had been a sign of mourning in old folk lore, indicative of desertion if not of death. Dido had stood with a willow in her hand while she watched for her faithless lover upon the sea shore. Desdemona had sung 'Willow, willow,' while she grieved over the inexplicable change in her husband before he killed her. Willow had been planted in memory of a brave and generous woman who had died unjustly, thus changing the chateau's name from Chateau de Valprès to Chateau des Saules.

Halcyon turned away with a deep sigh. She too wore an invisible crown of willow. Though not exactly deserted, she had lost her love and was going out into the wilderness to try to exorcise its memory. Vainly, she thought wryly, for she would never see a weeping willow again without recalling that dark attractive figure lying in the shade of one who had wrought such havoc in her life.

Halcyon followed the course of the Loire by bus, train and boat, striving to still a consuming restlessness, her aroused emotions clamouring for some release. She passed the great chateaux where the river bed was shallowest, and the water ran sluggishly awaiting the replenishment of the autumn rains. There they were, the one-time magnificent homes of the aristocracy of France, now become museums, schools or even institutions. She traversed the Val d'Anjou, cradle of the most romantic kings who had ever sat on the English throne, from Henry II, the first Angevin king, who had brought law and order to a war-torn country though he was more usually remembered for his domestic strife, to Richard III who had died upon Bosworth field. She slept at night in humble inns or for preference cottages that advertised a room to let. Though she won many curious glances she was not molested. She had about her an aloof air, as if she were not quite of this world, and indeed she was so absorbed in her own thoughts, nothing made much impact. Sometimes the older and more superstitious peasants crossed themselves as she went by.

Finally she wandered into South Brittany and at the little fishing village of Le Croissic she came to a halt. It was situated on a creek that ran down to the sea, and she liked the cobbled streets and tall grey houses, the red sails of the fishing boats and the gnarled patient faces of its inhabitants. She found accommodation in a clean but bare apartment house, run by a Breton widow, simple but shrewd, whose tariff was moderate, and there at last she found peace. Occasionally coach loads of tourists came out from nearby La Baule to clatter through the streets, but they did not linger after buying a few souvenirs, for there was not much to see. Halcyon liked to go out in the early morning and walk down to the red rocks that edged the coast, or stand on the quay to watch the catch of multi-coloured herrings unloaded, so much brighter in hue than they afterwards became on the fishmongers' slabs. During the day she worked upon her novel. At first she found difficulty in concentrating, but gradually she picked up the threads and became absorbed in it. Thus she was able to banish Raoul from her thoughts. Only waking in the hour of the first daylight, she was assailed by a desolate sense of loss and had difficulty in restraining her tears.

The novel was completed with its essential happy ending, hero and heroine in each other's arms after their many vicissitudes. Halcyon despatched it to her publishers and studied the calendar. The days had slipped by in an almost timeless interlude and her father would be returning to Gracedieu. She hoped he had produced some good pictures worthy of an exhibition. He had friends in Paris who would help him if they were interested in his new work. She must persuade him to contact them, for he was hopeless at any sort of organisation, and she would have to induce him to be practical. She hoped fervently also that he had lost Louis in Provence. She had no wish to encounter him again.

She found she was sorry to leave the sanctuary of Le Croissic. Here she had found peace and learned resignation. It would not be easy to return to Le Nid with all its associations, but she did not intend to stay there for long and there would be so much to do arranging for their removal to the capital she would have no time for repining. She supposed she would also have to think of a theme for a new book, but she was determined the setting would not be in France this time, and definitely not the Empire period.

When she arrived back in Gracedieu, she found her father was there before her. She had left the key with a neighbour, so he had been able to get in, and his voice hailed her from the studio as she opened the front door.

'Hal, at last! Where the deuce have you been? I was beginning to think I would have to go to the police to trace you. I've been home two days, and of course I rang up Madame de Valprès, but she said you'd gone off into the blue ages ago, without leaving an address.'

He came to the door of the studio, a tall figure bronzed by the sun of the Midi. 'What possessed you to go away?'

'Madame's former secretary recovered, so I was a bit redundant,' Halcyon explained vaguely. 'So I took the opportunity of having a wander around. I didn't expect you so soon.'

Felix's anxiety, if indeed he had been anxious, which she rather doubted was soon appeased. He had not minded having to wait upon himself in her absence, he was quite capable of attending to his own

167

needs in a slapdash manner, but he needed her appreciation of the work he had done in Provence and the Camargue. He took her by the arm and drew her into the studio where he had displayed his pictures.

'There, what do you think of them?' he asked proudly.

She was impressed; his talent had grown in strength and power. Less futuristic than usual, the subjects were recognisable for what they were, and his canvases fairly glowed with light and heat. Some of the Camargue pictures with cloud-filled skies reflected in watery lagoons conveyed a nostalgic atmosphere, and were beautiful. He told her proudly that he had already had substantial offers from collectors in Nîmes and Arles, but he first wished to show them in an exhibition, his own exhibition if possible, in Paris.

'It'll be a little expensive,' she pointed out, 'but perhaps we can manage it.'

'Of course we can, and I'll be able to fleece Dubois again. He wants another portrait of Mariette, this time in her wedding gown.'

Halcyon's heart gave a hard throb. She had expected no less, but this blunt reference to Mariette's wedding dress hit her.

'So Monsieur Dubois recovered,' she remarked, realising that she had had no news from Gracedieu for nearly six weeks. 'When I left he was seriously ill.'

'Was he? I haven't seen him, of course, I found a letter from him about the portrait when I got back, asking me to phone him. He sounded spry enough when I rang up, even the fire at the chateau did not seem to have upset him.'

Halcyon stared at him. 'The ... fire?' she faltered.

'Didn't you hear about it? I believe it was reported in *Le Matin*.'

She shook her head.

'I've been out in the wilds, and I didn't read any newspapers.' She had wanted to dissociate herself from any mundane happenings while she concentrated upon her book. 'Was it badly damaged? Is it habitable?'

'I shouldn't think so. The walls are still standing, it would take more than a fire to destroy them, but the interior was gutted.'

'When did it happen?'

'About a week ago, I understand.'

After Raoul would have proposed to Mariette and been accepted. She remembered when she had last seen him escorting the girl out of the salon at Bellevue, and his proprietorial air as he had ushered her to the car. Then it had seemed he had been well on the way to fulfil his strongest desire, to be master of the Chateau des Saules. But Pierre Dubois had recovered and was still in control, while the chateau was a ruin, so he had gained nothing through his mercenary engagement. In a sense it was rough justice, but she was too generous to think of that. Instead her heart was full of pity for him; he did not love Mariette, and he would take the loss of the chateau very hard.

'What caused it?' she asked.

'Friend Dubois was a bit too lavish with his electrical installations,' Felix told her cheerfully, seeming no whit disturbed by the catastrophe. 'It's a bit risky wiring those ancient monuments. They think some electrical fault was responsible for the blaze.'

Halcyon moistened her dry lips.

'Was ... was anyone hurt?'

For surely if Raoul had been on the scene he would have made some frantic endeavour to save the place. She dreaded to hear of some reckless action that had resulted in further tragedy.

'No. Luckily the family were away at the time at the seaside. If Dubois had been ill, I suppose they took him away to recuperate. André didn't discover the fire until it had got a firm hold, and of course after the hot weather we've been having everything was as dry as tinder. Nor was it easy to get water, the river being so low with the drought. Of course they tried to put it out, without success. The excitement in the village was tremendous, as you can imagine. Haven't had such an event for years. Since I've been back, I've heard nothing else but stories of the fire. They did their best to extinguish it, with incredible valour, according to their own accounts.' He laughed. 'But of course it was ages before a fire engine could arrive in this remote spot, and then it was too late.'

Halcyon stared absently at Felix's study of the Pont du Gard. It was done from an unusual angle, just one huge span reflected in the river. Even Madame de Valprès could not consider that banal, but her thoughts had winged again to Raoul. Where had he been when the conflagration had engulfed his beloved Chateau des Saules, and what was he thinking now that he had lost the heritage for which he was prepared to sacrifice so much? He would not be so caddish as to repudiate Mariette now she had been deprived of her most prized possession, Felix's mention of the wedding had proved that, but he must be feeling very bitter.

'The pictures in the gallery,' she said suddenly. 'Were any of them saved?'

'I doubt it. The gallery was an inferno by the time anybody got there. Certainly Mariette's portrait was lost, and I'm not upset about that, it was a sorry daub, and now Papa wants another.' He chuckled; evidently the destruction of the contents of the chateau did not disturb him in the least.

'I don't want to stay here,' Halcyon said abruptly. She could not bear to revive her memories.

'Neither do I,' Felix concurred. 'The Dubois will be at their Paris apartment for the wedding.' Halcyon winced inwardly. 'It is there they wish me to paint Mariette and it'll fit in nicely with my plans for an exhibition.'

Halcyon had no desire to renew contact with the Dubois family, but upon reflection saw no reason why she should have to do so. Only Felix would be invited to their apartment, and all they could afford for themselves would be some humble lodging far from the fashionable area where the family would be sure to be living, and it was improbable that in a big city like Paris she would encounter either them or Raoul.

So far Felix had not mentioned the de Valprès, except indirectly by reference to the wedding. She wondered if Madame had reconciled herself to the inevitable, and thought she would be a formidable mother-in-law if the bride were not to her liking. That, however, was Mariette's headache, and having a very good opinion of herself, no doubt she would be able to cope with Cécile. She did not wish to mention either Madame or her son to her father, fearing he would make some facetious comment about them. Raoul's present position would appeal to his puckish humour and he would laugh at his predicament, that of a man who was taking a woman he did not love to gain a home that was now a ruin.

But perhaps Raoul did have some *tendresse* for Mariette in spite of his criticisms, and it might have ripened into affection. She remembered how gentle he had been with her when she had come to him in her distress. Mariette was not unlovable and she would still have a substantial dowry. Raoul might be counting upon her money to rebuild the Chateau des Saules, which would be an expensive project.

Seeking a diversion from her unhappy thoughts, she asked what had become of Louis Perron.

'Oh, he's going out East,' Felix told her with amusement. 'Latched up with a gang of kindred spirits, flower people or whatever they call themselves nowadays. They were to trek across Asia Minor battening on native hospitality and hope to end up eventually in Nepal. I don't think we'll be seeing him again.'

Halcyon felt a twinge of compunction.

'Do you think he could have reformed?' she asked. 'Gone back to normal life if he'd had ... er ... sufficient inducement?'

'No,' Felix said decidedly. 'He's a weak man, and incapable of resolution.' He shot Halcyon a shrewd glance. 'Did he contemplate doing so?'

'Yes, when he was thinking of getting married,' Halcyon admitted frankly. 'Oh, Daddy, if I'd accepted him do you think I could have saved him?'

Felix whistled. 'So that's why he was going about looking like a broody hen.' He dropped his light manner and said seriously:

'At one time I thought he might be a good proposition for you, but now I realise he has no stability, and you were wise to refuse him. To marry in a crusading spirit is to kindle one's own hell, and I don't believe any woman can reform a man permanently, certainly not one like poor Louis, so you needn't reproach yourself.' He sighed. 'One drifter in the family is quite enough, but at least I've always been true to my art, and now my dedication is about to pay dividends.' He glanced with satisfaction at his collection of paintings.

'They're better than anything else you've ever done,'

Halcyon was enthusiastic. 'You've got genius, Daddy, that Louis lacked.'

'Very kind of you to say so,' Felix observed a little drily. 'It's my justification.'

Looking at her pensive face, he noted that she looked paler and thinner than when he had seen her last. Not wholly insensitive, he suspected some emotional turmoil had driven her away, but he shrank from any confidences. Young girls were always falling in and out of love, and she would soon get over whatever it was. He remembered de Valprès had paid her some attention, but he had warned her not to take him seriously. She must know that he would expect a dowry, and presumably he had decided to marry the Dubois girl at last. Monsieur Dubois had been too eager to talk about the portrait during their phone call to mention the bridegroom, but it could not be anybody else.

He had always considered his daughter was a sensible young woman, and she would not waste time moping over that young *roué*.

He said brightly:

'Let's get out of here as soon as possible. Perhaps you will see Monsieur Blum about it? I don't expect he'll raise any difficulty about curtailing the tenancy, he didn't consider we were paying enough rent. A bit of fun in Paris is what you need, you're looking positively peaky. If I have a success you'll be besieged with admirers with your looks.'

Halcyon knew this was a clumsy effort at consolation, and smiled wryly.

'I'm looking forward to going,' she told him, 'but I don't want any admirers. They can be tiresome and I don't want to marry, ever. I shall devote myself to a literary career. Fictitious people are so much easier to manage than real ones.'

'You like to manipulate the strings? Well, I don't want to lose you, darling, and since you're here what about a cup of tea? I brought in some milk and sugar and I haven't had a decent cuppa since I left Grace-dieu.'

She had gone straight into the studio upon her arrival, her father being too impatient to show his creations to permit her to dawdle. Now she collected her worn suitcase and typewriter and dumped them in her bedroom, thinking the bedding would have to be aired and wondered if Felix had thought to turn on the electricity, but of course he must have done since he had been in residence for two days.

She looked round the little kitchen with wistful eyes while she waited for the kettle to boil, almost she expected to see Raoul's tall figure darkening the back entrance, and hear Saracen's impatient champing outside. He had been so charming to them during those first days, and she wondered a little vaguely what would have happened if he had not caught her with Louis and been so affronted. Nothing different, she supposed, he had by his own admission only used the incident as a pretext to break away from her, and had hoped, yes, actually dared to hope that she was the fickle creature she had appeared to be. The kettle boiled and she made the tea. She could not get away from Le Nid too soon to please her.

The long spell of golden summer weather broke with thunderstorms and heavy rain. Felix talked gaily of all they were going to do in Paris, but it was Halcyon who booked accommodation for them and packed his precious canvases. She gave in their notice to Monsieur Blum, who could not disguise his satisfaction, now he would be able to obtain what he considered was a fair rent for the cottage. Raoul, he disclosed, was in Paris and unlikely to return for some time. Halcyon left his office not knowing if she were relieved or sorry. She had half dreaded, half longed to see him again if it were only in the village street, now she knew that she would in all probability never see him again, for whatever her father did, she was determined to have no contact with the Dubois. She was anxious to break the connection entirely, for she must stop herself from thinking about Raoul, and she tried to persuade Felix not to paint Mariette's picture.

'We can manage without the money and you know you hate that sort of assignment,' she pointed out.

But Felix was contrary, he seemed to have conceived a liking for Pierre Dubois and was determined to keep in with the family.

'Their friends will support my exhibition,' he declared.

'They aren't artistic people.'

'They'll buy what's fashionable, and I've a hunch I'm going to be the rage,' he said confidently.

Halcyon thought he was probably right, his paintings were going to create a sensation and since he was determined to paint Mariette's portrait she would have to resign herself to the inevitable. Unfortunately he seemed really excited about it and persisted in discussing it with her. He had obtained the information that Mariette was to be married in wild silk and lace, and he was interested in how to treat the materials to show their texture.

'If only it were you who were going to wear it,' he said with unconscious cruelty. 'Your face is so much more interesting than hers.'

He never referred to the bridegroom, but whether out of tact or indifference, Halcyon was not sure, and she herself never mentioned the de Valprès, though the family was constantly in her thoughts. Since the wedding was to be in Paris, the villagers took no interest in it, they were still mulling over the fire, which touched them far more nearly.

Nor did she ever run into Madame de Valprès, and she concluded she too was in Paris.

They had been back little more than a week when their arrangements for moving had been completed.

The day before they left was one of alternate sun and shower, with a breeze blowing. In the early evening Felix announced he was going down to the bistro to take leave of his cronies in the village, and Halcyon was left alone.

She felt a return of the old restlessness that had driven her to Le Croissic coupled with a strong urge to visit the chateau. She had several times felt curious about it, for though she could see the towers from the village and they looked the same as usual, she knew there must be considerable devastation down below them. She would like to see for herself the extent of the damage and judge whether Raoul had any hope of renovating it.

This evening would be her last chance to view it, and she felt almost irresistibly drawn towards it. Afterwards she was to wonder if this was not a case of thought transference, but then she had no idea of what she would find there.

Sometimes she had hated that stone pile, which had come between her and ... what? She had no real reason to believe that Raoul would have married her even if he had not been obsessed by it, so it was absurd to regard it as an enemy. The descendants of the Comte de Valprès came of noble stock and did not marry dowerless artists' daughters, however much in love with them they might be, and she had always doubted the genuineness of Raoul's feelings for her. However much he might be drawn towards her he would expect to make a more suitable alliance when it came to marriage.

True, his mother had declared that he was attached to her, and she would rather her son married her than Mariette, but she was, as Raoul had said, a devious woman, and it was quite possible she had meant to use Halcyon to detach Raoul from the Dubois, but would not countenance a marriage. She had been confident that the girl would be unable to resist her own emotions and would consent to a less regular union. When Halcyon had failed in the purpose for which she had been engaged, she had seemed quite pleased to let her go.

However, Raoul had put himself out of reach, and before finally closing that chapter of her life, Halcyon yielded to her desire to take her leave of the Chateau des Saules.

She put on a white raincoat, somewhat the worse for wear, over slacks and pullover and tied a scarf over her hair. She walked through the village, across the narrow neck of land that connected it with the Chateau des Saules, and along the gravelled drive towards the front entrance. There she stopped, appalled. The twin towers were as they had always been, and the façade between them still stood, with its fine pillared entrance door, but behind it all was desolation. The roof of the gallery had caved in and the setting sun illuminated eyeless windows whence the glass had fallen. A massive wooden fence had been erected around the building, for it was unsafe, on which its dangerous nature was proclaimed in scarlet lettering.

'*Attention! Danger! Interdit!*'

The beautiful lawns and gardens in front of the chateau were trampled and sodden where the over-enthusiastic villagers had milled around the flaming edifice and the tardy fire engine had manoeuvred and dripped water from its hoses.

Halcyon turned away, sick at heart, wishing she had not come. The Chateau des Saules had withstood sieges and assaults for centuries, and it had survived the fighting in two world wars, but the final destruction had come from within. An overloaded electrical system and too many inflammable modern furnishings.

The cypress hedge, though singed in places, still stood between the desecrated gardens and the Roman bath. Halcyon picked her way through the familiar gap in them, believing that that at least would be untouched. But she found she was wrong, for the water had been sucked from it to use against the flames and the marble rim was mired with mud and filth. The spring was slowly refilling it, but the once clear water was full of debris. Only the willow trees were the same, extending their long fronds downwards to seek their reflection in the sullied pool. But they were trembling at the approach of autumn, their delicate green turning to yellow, cascades of leaves already falling to add to the rubbish in the bath. Again Halcyon wished she had not come. She would have preferred to remember it as it had been on that summer's day when she had swum away from Raoul, a gracious, charming spot. Now it was a desolate ruin, and her last view of it would always be superimposed upon her first one, and much more strongly, for this utter desolation was much more impressive than its former smiling prettiness. Never more would the gay umbrellas be unfurled above its marble paving, for the marble had cracked anew and it would cost a fortune to restore it. Together with the chateau it would become a haunted place, legends would spring up about it, already there were some, and it would be shunned by the superstitious villagers.

Halcyon looked up at the lowering sky, the setting sun threw lurid beams between the massed clouds, and she shivered, for the breeze was cool, its cold breath on her cheeks was like a whisper from another world, the spirits of long-dead de Valprès who were coming back to claim their own.

Resisting an impulse to run, for she knew she was being absurdly fanciful, Halcyon moved away from the rim of the pool, and fixed her thoughts upon the mundane details of the morrow, to counteract the place's eerie atmosphere. Then all would be bustle and confusion as they made their final preparations for departure early in the morning, and by evening they would be settled in Paris. This was her last moment of solitude, her final farewell to the most memorable experience in her short life.

' 'Alcyone!'

She started violently. Now surely the spot must be haunted. Only one voice possessed that deep vibrant note, and only one person had used the classical version of her name. She had never expected to see him again, nor hear the familiar inflection. But Raoul was not dead like his ancestors, he was away in Paris, paying court to Mariette Dubois, and her imagination was playing tricks with her. She turned apprehensive eyes towards the group of willows, and gave a gasp. Parting them, holding a drooping wand in either hand, was the figure of Raoul de Valprès. His dark sweater and trousers merged with the shadows beneath the trees, while a lingering shaft of pale light touched his face with strange luminosity, in which the eye sockets were

dark pits. He looked unearthly and Halcyon gave a
strangled cry of terror and despair. In that awful moment she believed that something must have happened
to Raoul and she was seeing his ghost. She sank down
upon the muddied rim of the basin in a little white
heap.

CHAPTER TEN

'How many more times will I have to come to your rescue?' a familiar voice was enquiring. 'Whatever upset you this time? I see nothing venomous or dangerous around, and there is not even a bit of broken glass.'

'Oh, Raoul!' Shakily Halcyon put up a hand and touched his cheek, to reassure herself. 'So you're alive! I ... I thought you were your ghost.'

'I have not been reduced to haunting the Chateau des Saules yet,' he told her with a laugh. 'But where in the name of *le bon Dieu* have you been all this while? Nobody seemed to know where you had gone.'

With the realisation that he was flesh and blood, Halcyon recovered her nerve. She found that Raoul had raised her from the ground and was holding her against himself. Very decisively, she disengaged herself and moved a few feet away from him.

'Thank you,' she said primly. 'But I no longer need support. It gave me a shock seeing you so unexpectedly. What are you doing here?'

'The same as you, I suppose. Looking at the wreck of the poor old Chateau. It is a sad sight, *n'est-ce pas?*'

'It is indeed.'

'*Eh bien*, it has had its day,' he said philosophically. 'It will not cause any more heartbreaks.'

She was surprised by his cool acceptance of the chateau's destruction; she would have expected him to be in despair.

'But why are you here?' she repeated. 'You're supposed to be in Paris.'

'Am I? Why should you think that?'

'I was told so by your agent.'

'Actually I was, but I left this morning. Where have you been, 'Alcyone? I scoured the country for you.'

So Madame had been right, her flight had roused the hunter in him, but to what purpose? He was about to marry Mariette.

'I went away to find a peaceful spot to finish my novel,' she said quietly. 'It wasn't possible here. There were too many distractions.'

'And is it completed, happy ending and all?' he asked mockingly.

'Yes,' she was almost curt.

'*Bon*. Now perhaps you will give me a happy ending to my story, *ma petite*,' he said insinuatingly.

'I'm afraid that is not possible,' she returned stiffly. 'If you mean, what I think you mean, I can only tell you, as we say in England, that having made your bed you must lie on it.'

'With you?'

'Oh, really, Raoul!' she exclaimed in exasperation, realising that she had used an unfortunate metaphor. As Mariette's marriage was the talk of the neighbourhood, he was showing very bad taste by trying to flirt with her. She went on quickly to divert him. 'We're leaving for Paris tomorrow, we've found an apartment there, and my father is going to paint another portrait of Mariette.'

'How delightful!'

'In her wedding gown,' Halcyon said with emphasis.

'I am sure the lucky bridegroom will appreciate his efforts.'

'You didn't admire the last picture. You said Daddy had caught her silly simper, or some such, which I thought at the time was a bit off under the circumstances, but perhaps you've learnt to appreciate her upon closer acquaintanceship. I believe she's a nice girl at heart.'

She spoke wildly and at random; his nearness was working its old magic upon her and his inconsequential manner was irritating. He must have no regard for her feelings at all, for he would know by now that her heart was his, and he was being cruel to tease her.

'I think you are under a misapprehension,' Raoul told her.

'How could I be? It was perfectly obvious when Mariette came for you when her father was ill what you intended to do.'

Raoul drew a long breath. 'I am forgetting you have been out of circulation for so long,' he observed. 'Events have changed, my little one.'

'Yes, the chateau has been burned out. Too bad when you'd sold yourself to gain it.'

'That you should dare to say such a thing to me!'

She could not see his face in the gathering dusk, for the sun had slipped below the horizon and the heavy clouds were causing an early nightfall, but she knew from his tone she had touched him on the raw. He sounded furious.

'It's true,' she said stubbornly.

'It is not true. Of course I had to go with Mariette when she appealed to me for help. She and her mother were both nearly hysterical. Someone had to take command.'

'That was what you had always wanted, wasn't it? To be in command of the Chateau des Saules, to lord it where your ancestors ruled, but all you've got is a ruin.'

She spoke with a sort of dreary triumph for the chateau had been her real rival, not the woman.

Raoul uttered an imprecation. 'You always were a provoking little witch,' he said angrily. His voice softened and changed. 'I will never forget you as you were when I first saw you on this very spot, Psyche risen from her bath. I told you then I had felt a *coup de foudre*, but you did not know what I meant, did you, *ma mie*? Nor did I fully recognise its significance. It was only later when I met you again that I knew I had fallen in love—yes, really in love, and for the first time, with you and at first sight. Oh, I fought against it ... and you.' She sensed though she could not see his rueful smile. 'It was so ... inconvenient, but it was no use.'

They both fell silent, recalling the idyllic days of their early meetings. Then Halcyon gave a sharp sigh.

'That's all very nice to know,' she said a little tartly, 'but it's a bit late in the day to bring it up now.' She tied her scarf more securely under her chin. 'It is nearly dark and Daddy will be wondering what's become of me, so I will wish you *adieu*, Monsieur de Valprès, and it really must be *adieu* this time.'

'No, 'Alcyone, I will not permit that.'

'I'm afraid you will have to. Or are you so insensitive that you expect me to dance at your wedding? Goodbye, Raoul.'

She turned to go, anxious to escape before she betrayed the anguish and despair that had suddenly assailed her. She had managed very well up to this point, but if she stayed longer, she would break down, throw herself into his arms, beg him not to put her out of his life altogether, and that she would accept any position if he could spare her a few crumbs of affection apart from Mariette. She would like to have run, but that was impossible in the dark and the marble beneath her feet was slippery. She had taken a few cautious steps when his voice arrested her.

'Whom do you imagine I am going to marry, *petite imbécile?*'

'I don't imagine anything,' she said indignantly. 'I was told as soon as I returned that preparations were being made for Mariette's wedding. I even known what her dress is going to be made of.'

'Mariette is going to be married, but she is not going to marry me.'

'What?' Halcyon spun round to face him, but he was only a dark shadow confronting her. 'You're not trying to deceive me?' she asked uncertainly.

'*Chérie*, why should I do that? Had you stayed instead of running away, you would have heard all about it. During her father's illness, I had several long talks with Mariette. She no more wished to marry me than I did her. Her fancy was fixed upon that gawk who deputised for me in Murat's uncomfortable uniform. *Chacun à son goût*, but at least he was obliging. It was her father who was pressing her to marry me, and she was a dutiful daughter, as I tried to be a dutiful son.' He laughed sardonically. 'We decided we were both making a terrible mistake and we would follow our hearts, for we knew best what was good for us. When he was sufficiently recovered to be told, Dubois sanctioned his daughter's marriage to the pseudo-Murat. It is he who is to be her bridegroom.'

Halcyon heard his words, but had difficulty in assimilating them. Could he be speaking the truth? Yet he was here and not in Paris. She said uncertainly:

'I suppose you didn't mind relinquishing Mariette

since the chateau was burnt.'

'How can you say such a thing!' he flashed.

'Well, it seems so strange ... you were so set ...'

'Actually we jilted each other long before the chateau was on fire,' he said more calmly, then with a burst of emotion, ''Alcyone, there are times when I could strangle you. After that night at Bellevue surely you knew I would find a way to come to you?'

'That night you told me how much you resented my interference in your life,' she retorted.

'Did I? But I had known for a long time I wanted you more than any chateau. *Alors*, I had made a promise to my father, and that was the obstacle. Now I am absolved in every way. 'Alcyone, will you be my wife?'

Words she had never expected to hear and even now she doubted if he were in earnest.

'I have no *dot*,' she murmured.

'*Tiens*, as if that mattered! Oh, *mon Dieu, chérie*, why are you stalling? These past weeks when you could not be found I nearly went frantic.'

'Yet you were away when I returned.'

'Urgent business took me to Paris. I had no idea when you would return or even if you intended to do so. Did you expect me to sit on your doorstep for six solid weeks? I did very nearly.'

'Such an uncomfortable seat,' she observed with laughter in her voice.

'Perhaps not literally,' he confessed. '*Eh bien*, Blum telephoned to me to tell me you were back and had given up the tenancy of the cottage. I came as quickly as possible, but it seems I am only just in time. What an elusive creature you are, *ma mie*.'

His voice was warm and vibrant, but he was only a slightly darker shadow than those beneath the trees. He appeared to have no substance and fear gripped her that she was experiencing a fantasy such as she had sometimes woven in her daydreams. She had lost consciousness when she had fallen on the edge of the bath, and she was still not fully herself. He could not really have asked her to be his wife.

'I think I am dreaming,' she said. 'You didn't actually ask me to marry you, did you?'

'I did, and perhaps this will convince you of my reality.'

The shadow became a very solid man with strong arms that were both possessive and tender and lips that were warm and insistent, pressing upon her own.

Some time later they picked their uncertain way back towards the village, stumbling over unidentifiable objects in the dark. When they had reached the connecting neck of land, Halcyon withdrew from Raoul's encircling arm and looked back.

A broad band of yellow light above the horizon gave a valediction to the dying day, below the massed clouds. Against it the towers of the chateau were silhouetted, black and stark. She said tentatively:

'I suppose you could buy it cheap now, Raoul, and you could possibly rebuild it.'

'I do not want it,' he returned. 'It has already cost me too much; I nearly lost you. I have come to believe that my poor father was greatly mistaken, it is wiser to let the past die, for we belong to a new age and we should look forward and not back.'

'But you told me once you belonged to the Chateau des Saules with your ancestors.'

'They are dust and I am alive. I belong to you, *chérie*, as you do to me, and Bellevue to both of us. I think it will make a happier home for our children than that old chateau.'

The clouds descended, obliterating the last of the light, and the towers were shrouded in gloom. Hand in hand Raoul and Halcyon walked towards the lights of the village, while the future beckoned to them with the promise of true happiness among the vineyards in the hills.

NEW!

HARLEQUIN
SUPERROMANCE

LOVE'S EMERALD FLAME
WILLA LAMBERT

A Contemporary Love Story

The steaming jungle of Peru was the stage
for their love. Diana Green, a spirited
and beautiful young journalist, who became
a willing pawn in a dangerous game...
and Sloane Hendriks, a lonely desperate
man, driven by a secret he would
reveal to no one.

Love's Emerald Flame is the second stunning novel in
this timely new series of modern love stories—
HARLEQUIN SUPERROMANCES.

Longer, exciting, sensual and dramatic, these
compelling new books are for you—the woman of today!

Watch for HARLEQUIN SUPERROMANCE #2, Love's Emerald
Flame, in November wherever paperback books are sold
or order your copy from

Harlequin Reader Service

In U.S.A.
MPO Box 707
Niagara Falls, NY 14302

In Canada
649 Ontario St.
Stratford, Ont. N5A 6W2

Here's how to get your volume NOW!

MAIL IN	$	GET
2 SPECIAL PROOF-OF-PURCHASE SEALS*	PLUS $1 U.S.	ONE BOOK
5 SPECIAL PROOF-OF-PURCHASE SEALS*	PLUS 50¢ U.S.	ONE BOOK
8 SPECIAL PROOF-OF-PURCHASE SEALS*	FREE	ONE BOOK

*Special proof-of-purchase seal from inside back cover of all specially marked Harlequin "Let Your Imagination Fly Sweepstakes" volumes. No other proof-of-purchase accepted.

ORDERING DETAILS:

Print your name, address, city, state or province, zip or postal code on the coupon below or a plain 3"x 5" piece of paper and together with the special proof-of-purchase seals and check or money order (no stamps or cash please) as indicated. Mail to:

HARLEQUIN
ROMANCE TREASURY
BOOK OFFER
P.O. BOX 1399
MEDFORD, N.Y. 11763, U.S.A.

Make check or money order payable to: Harlequin Romance Treasury Offer. Allow 3 to 4 weeks for delivery.

Special offer expires: June 30, 1981.

PLEASE PRINT

Name

Address

Apt. No.

City

State/Prov.

Zip/Postal Code

Let Your Imagination Fly Sweepstakes

Rules and Regulations:

NO PURCHASE NECESSARY

1. Enter the Let Your Imagination Fly Sweepstakes 1, 2 or 3 as often as you wish. Mail each entry form separately bearing sufficient postage. Specify the sweepstake you wish to enter on the outside of the envelope. Mail a completed entry form or, your name, address, and telephone number printed on a plain 3"x 5" piece of paper to:
HARLEQUIN LET YOUR IMAGINATION FLY SWEEPSTAKES,
P.O. BOX 1280, MEDFORD, N.Y. 11763 U.S.A.

2. Each completed entry form must be accompanied by 1 Let Your Imagination Fly proof-of-purchase seal from the back inside cover of specially marked Let Your Imagination Fly Harlequin books (or the words "Let Your Imagination Fly" printed on a plain 3" x 5" piece of paper. Specify by number the Sweepstakes you are entering on the outside of the envelope.

3. The prize structure for each sweepstake is as follows:

Sweepstake 1 - North America
Grand Prize winner's choice: a one-week trip for two to either Bermuda; Montreal, Canada; or San Francisco. 3 Grand Prizes will be awarded (min. approx. retail value $1,375. U.S., based on Chicago departure) and 4,000 First Prizes: scarves by nik nik, worth $14. U.S. each. All prizes will be awarded.

Sweepstake 2 - Caribbean
Grand Prize winner's choice: a one-week trip for two to either Nassau, Bahamas; San Juan, Puerto Rico; or St. Thomas,Virgin Islands. 3 Grand Prizes will be awarded. (Min. approx. retail value $1,650. U.S., based on Chicago departure) and 4,000 First Prizes: simulated diamond pendants by Kenneth Jay Lane, worth $15. U.S. each. All prizes will be awarded.

Sweepstake 3 - Europe
Grand Prize winner's choice: a one-week trip for two to either London, England; Frankfurt, Germany; Paris, France; or Rome, Italy. 3 Grand Prizes will be awarded. (Min. approx. retail value $2,800. U.S., based on Chicago departure) and 4,000 First Prizes: 1/2 oz. bottles of perfume, BLAZER by Anne Klein. (Retail value over $30. U.S.). All prizes will be awarded.

Grand trip prizes will include coach round-trip airfare for two persons from the nearest commercial airport serviced by Delta Air Lines to the city as designated in the prize, double occupancy accommodation at a first- class or medium hotel, depending on vacation, and $500. U.S. spending money. Departure taxes, visas, passports, ground transportation to and from airports will be the responsibility of the winners.

4. To be eligible, Sweepstakes entries must be received as follows:
Sweepstake 1 Entries received by February 28, 1981
Sweepstake 2 Entries received by April 30, 1981
Sweepstake 3 Entries received by June 30, 1981
Make sure you enter each Sweepstake separately since entries will not be carried forward from one Sweepstake to the next.

The odds of winning will be determined by the number of entries received in each of the three sweepstakes. Canadian residents, in order to win any prize, will be required to first correctly answer a time-limited skill-testing question, to be posed by telephone, at a mutually convenient time.

5. Random selections to determine Sweepstake 1, 2 or 3 winners will be conducted by Lee Krost Associates, an independent judging organization whose decisions are final. Only one prize per family, per sweepstake. Prizes are non-transferable and non-refundable and no substitutions will be allowed. Winners will be responsible for any applicable federal, state and local taxes. Trips must be taken during normal tour periods before June 30, 1982. Reservations will be on a space-available basis. Airline tickets are non-transferable, non-refundable and non-redeemable for cash.

6. The Let Your Imagination Fly Sweepstakes is open to all residents of the United States of America and Canada, (excluding the Province of Quebec) except employees and their immediate families of Harlequin Enterprises Ltd., its advertising agencies, Marketing & Promotion Group Canada Ltd. and Lee Krost Associates, Inc., the independent judging company. Winners may be required to furnish proof of eligibility. Void wherever prohibited or restricted by law. All federal, state, provincial and local laws apply.

7. For a list of trip winners, send a stamped, self-addressed envelope to:
Harlequin Trip Winners List, P.O. Box 1401, MEDFORD, N.Y. 11763 U.S.A.
Winners lists will be available after the last sweepstake has been conducted and winners determined.
NO PURCHASE NECESSARY.

Let Your Imagination Fly Sweepstakes

OFFICIAL ENTRY FORM

Please enter me In Sweepstake No. _____

Please print:
Name

Address

Apt. No.   City

State/   Zip/Postal
Prov.   Code

Telephone No.   area code
                 (   )

MAIL TO:
HARLEQUIN LET YOUR
IMAGINATION FLY SWEEPSTAKE No._____
P.O. BOX 1280,
MEDFORD, N.Y. 11763 U.S.A.
(Please specify by number, the Sweepstake you are entering.)